MURDER
IN THE
EXECUTIVE
MANSION

Also by Elliott Roosevelt

A Royal Murder
Murder in the East Room
New Deal for Death
Murder in the West Wing
Murder in the Red Room
The President's Man
A First-Class Murder
Murder in the Blue Room
Murder in the Rose Garden
Murder in the Oval Office
Murder at the Palace
The White House Pantry Murder
Murder at Hobcaw Barony
The Hyde Park Murder
Murder and the First Lady

Perfect Crimes (ed.)

MURDER IN THE EXECUTIVE MANSION

Elliott Roosevelt

St. Martin's Press
New York

Production Editor: David Stanford Burr

ISBN 0-312-13128-3

As always and forever to my wife, Patty

MURDER IN THE EXECUTIVE MANSION

The President of the United States woke earlier than his usual hour on the morning of Thursday, June 8, 1939. Although Mrs. Roosevelt characteristically tried to restrain displays of emotion, her husband was an outgoing, exuberant personality, for whom having fun was an important element of life. And this was a day when he expected to have fun.

"Bill Bullitt is a funny man!" he laughed.

He referred to William Bullitt, United States Ambassador to the Quai d' Orsay, Paris. Missy LeHand, his personal and private secretary, who sat at the foot of his bed in a light-blue nightgown and peignoir, pouring coffee, had handed him the pages—a long confidential communication from the ambassador. It was a set of detailed instructions about the amenities that must be provided for their Britannic Majesties, King George VI and Queen Elizabeth, on the occasion of their state visit to the White House, which was to begin today. The memorandum went into exhaustive detail, suggesting how furniture should be placed and what kinds of sheets and pillows should be put on the royal beds.

"Two hot water bottles for each bed!" the President guf-

fawed, plucking off his pince-nez. "In Washington in June?
Towels, washcloths, soap! Does Bill imagine we don't nor-
mally have towels, washcloths, and soap in the White
House?"

"Maybe he's heard about Mrs. Nesbitt," said Missy.

Henrietta Nesbitt was the Hudson River neighbor Mrs.
Roosevelt had brought to Washington to be official housekeeper in the White House. A more inept housekeeper for a
grand house could hardly have been imagined. She tried to
run the White House according to the standards of a rural
New York farmhouse—which suited the First Lady perfectly,
since Mrs. Roosevelt had no interest in elegant food and
drink, or indeed any other extravagant elegance in living.
Mrs. Nesbitt ran the White House most frugally, which was
exactly what the First Lady wanted from her. Mrs. Roosevelt
was keenly aware that congressional appropriations for the
White House were miserly and that any expenditures beyond
those mean appropriations had to be made up out of family
funds; so she appreciated Mrs. Nesbitt's ability to keep
mostly within the budget and not make exorbitant calls on
the dwindling Roosevelt family fortune.

"For this occasion we can go hog-wild," said the President.
"I'm calling in money from the State Department—and if you
want a joke, even from the Department of the Interior—to
fund an appropriate reception for the King and Queen of England. We can assure Bill Bullitt there will be soap in the
King's and Queen's bathroom. Even clean towels."

"And the toilets are indoors," said Missy.

"Most of them," the President laughed.

His tray was over his lap as he sat propped up against pillows. He loved a good breakfast, and even Mrs. Nesbitt's
kitchen could do the hearty breakfast he liked: ham and
eggs, toast with marmalade, and coffee. Missy's tray sat beside his feet. The morning newspapers were scattered

around the bed. He had scanned a few of them—the New York *Herald*, the New York *Times*, the Washington *Post*, the Baltimroe *Sun*. He would get to others later—the Chicago *Tribune* for laughs, together with one or two of the Hearst papers.

Missy stood to put his coffee on his tray. She leaned over to kiss him, and he put his arms around her and prolonged the kiss.

"Missy . . . I wish I could put a tiara on you, and half a ton of diamonds, and seat you beside the Queen—"

"Efdee," she interrupted. "I wouldn't trade this breakfast for a dozen state dinners."

He caressed her along the side of her neck. "God . . ." he murmured. "I'm going to die of the sweats. Cutaway coat, waistcoat, striped pants, all wool . . . In a Washington summer!"

"You could have—"

"No. As you are painfully aware, I've worked out every element of the protocol. I've done it personally because I can't exaggerate the importance of this visit. Everything has to go smoothly. I can't have British newspapers suggesting the royal couple were in any way slighted. I want both peoples, the American and British, to see this as a triumph of friendship."

"It will be," Missy said gently.

The President stared skeptically at his formal clothes, on hangers hooked over his closet door. "Yes . . ." he said. "It's going to be a *grand* day!"

By the time the First Lady arrived, the President and Missy had finished their breakfasts. The President had finished scanning newspapers and was reading a stack of letters and memos, dictating replies to Missy. His first cigarette of the morning was in its holder, smoking in his hand as he dictated. Missy, still in her nightgown and peignoir, scribbled on a steno pad.

Mrs. Roosevelt knocked discreetly on the door and waited to be invited to enter. "Come in, Babs," said the President.

Although the President had wakened early, Mrs. Roosevelt had wakened earlier and had been out riding in Rock Creek Park on her horse, Dot. She was dressed in riding clothes: jacket with white shirt and necktie, jodhpurs, and riding boots. Her hair was fastened down by a yellow silk band. If anything could generate exhilaration in the First Lady, it was riding in early morning; and when she entered the President's bedroom she was still flushed and animated.

"If you'd been thrown, I'd have had no First Lady to greet the King and Queen," said the President, mock sternly.

"If I'd broken an arm or a rib I could do my day's duties," said Mrs. Roosevelt. "A leg . . . Well, I don't know. On the other hand, Dot has never thrown me."

"Was Elinor with you?"

Mrs. Roosevelt nodded. He referred to Elinor Morgenthau, wife of the Secretary of the Treasury and lifelong friend. "And an army captain," said Mrs. Roosevelt. "There would have been someone to pick me up."

"Thank God for small blessings," said the President.

"How have you resolved the problem of the chairs?" asked Mrs. Roosevelt. She referred to the fact that at White House dinners the President and First Lady always sat in special high-back armchairs, everyone else in comfortable but less regal chairs.

"We will sit in equal chairs," said the President. "I've ordered two more chairs to match ours. The King, the Queen, you, and I will sit at dinner in identical chairs."

"Then what of the notion that the King must be served thirty seconds before anyone else?"

"I've given instructions," said the President, "that the King and I are to be served simultaneously, after which you and the Queen will be served simultaneously."

Mrs. Roosevelt smiled. "Do we live in a real world?" she asked. "I mean, do we live in a world where things like this are really important?"

"I would guess," said the President, "that they are not important to King George or Queen Elizabeth but are important to a very great many other people, who will watch and remember and talk, talk, talk forever after—all of which will be the subject of endless commentary in the press."

"Yes," said the First Lady. "I like to think about what one of our neighbors once said— Which one was it? Do you remember? Anyway, she said there is an advantage in not being *too* good a housekeeper. That advantage is that your guests will feel more comfortable as they realize how much better they are than you are. I wager the King and Queen are this moment worrying about what faux pas they may make. If we make one or two, they will feel more at ease. It can't be easy to be royalty and to be expected to be absolutely correct about everything on every occasion."

The President clapped his hands. "Bravo, Babs! You put me in mind of the Yosemite park ranger who had to greet Albert, King of the Belgians, a few years ago. He'd been carefully coached about what he was to say, but when the time came he forgot it all and just thrust out his hand and said, 'Howdy, King.' King Albert loved it!"

"I imagine it was one of the most memorable moments of King Albert's visit," said Mrs. Roosevelt.

"Yes. Yes . . . But we don't have much time. I've got to get myself installed in that wool suit very shortly. We must not be late. I don't think the King and Queen would love it if their train came in and we weren't there to greet them."

* * *

The First Lady had given her secretary Malvina Thompson—known to everyone as Tommy—chief responsibility for the many details of her schedule during the royal visit. As Mrs. Roosevelt changed from her riding habit into a dressing gown, Tommy reviewed with her the agenda for the next several hours.

"Has Lucinda reviewed with Missy the seating arrangements for the luncheon?" asked Mrs. Roosevelt.

"I understand she has," said Tommy.

"Maybe we had better call her up here and make sure."

Tommy picked up the telephone and told the operator to ring Lucinda Robinson, a young woman who had been working for the past year as assistant to Edith Benham Helm, social secretary to the First Lady. By the time Mrs. Roosevelt had bathed and was dressed in a slip, the young woman had come up from her office in the East Wing on the ground floor.

The First Lady had learned to appreciate Lucinda Robinson for her intelligent attention to detail. Planning for the royal visit was the kind of thing the young woman did best. She had a special talent for organizing. What was more, she had no antipathy for long hours at what had to be dull work. She was a graduate of Saint Olaf College with a degree in modern languages, and she felt privileged to work in the White House.

Lucinda was a pudgy young woman, with a jowly round face. Her little mouth, lips tinted with pale lipstick, was like an O. People found it difficult to focus their eyes on hers, since hers were blurred by the thick lenses of her spectacles. Her complexion was pale and delicate, and her cheeks were pink. Her expression, typically, was dead serious, with a little frown.

She wore a modest dress, white with a pattern of tiny violet flowers and green leaves, cinched at the waist by a wide white patent-leather belt.

"I imagine the royal visit demands extra hours," said Mrs. Roosevelt. She sat at her dressing table but could see Lucinda's face in the mirror. "When we leave for New York, you should take a long weekend off."

"I am enjoying it," said Lucinda soberly.

"Be sure to be available this afternoon," said Mrs. Roosevelt. "I will present you to their royal majesties."

"Oh, I—"

"Yes, Lucinda. Tommy is going to meet them. Missy is going to meet them."

"Well, I have to wonder," said Lucinda quietly, "if at Buckingham Palace the King and Queen introduce members of their staff to important visitors."

"If they don't," said the First Lady, "I should imagine it is because hoary tradition stands in the way of their doing what they want to do. We are not bound by such traditions."

"I will be grateful," said Lucinda.

"So, then. Have you settled the seating arrangements for lunch?"

"The only problem has been with resisting the absolute demands to be included. The Secretary of This, the Secretary of That, Senator This and Congressman That . . ." She shook her head. Judges, generals, admirals . . . Even a bishop. Mrs. Helm has explained a score of times that the luncheon is for their majesties and no more than five guests outside the immediate family only. I've explained it a dozen times myself."

"And the menu?"

Lucinda shook her head somberly. "The President took one look at it and tore it to shreds, I'm afraid. No tuna salad, he said. Very firmly, ma'am. Very firmly."

"So what are we serving for lunch?"

"A platter of green and black olives, carrot sticks, celery, and quartered tomatoes, then rolled smoked salmon and stuffed eggs with mustard sauce. After that, a hot consommé. Then a green salad. Then Lobster Mayonnaise with potato salad. Followed by a cheese platter, including Brie and Port Salut. Peach pie, with or without ice cream. Then—"

"I am afraid he will discover all this is beyond Mrs. Nesbitt's capacities."

"Mrs. Nesbitt's function during the royal visit is limited to showing the imported chefs where things are," said Lucinda with no sign that she found the fact amusing. "What is more, the President said that if anyone brings New York State wine to the table, he will personally throw the bottles out the window."

"The President places a great deal of emphasis on such matters," said Mrs. Roosevelt.

"The dinners—" Lucinda shook her head. "I can't even pronounce the names of some of the dishes that will be served."

"Neither can I, probably," said the First Lady dryly. "Have you any problems I can help you with?"

"We are very nervous about it," said Lucinda.

"Don't be. I imagine we will find the royal couple very charming, forthcoming people."

The President and Mrs. Roosevelt met King George VI and Queen Elizabeth at Union Station. A Marine guard of honor stood at attention, smartly presenting arms as the royal couple emerged from the train.

The President, in a cutaway, was supported on the arm of Major General Edwin M. "Pa" Watson, in the white formal uniform of the United States Army. Mrs. Roosevelt wore a simple beige dress with white gloves and a broad, feathered straw hat. She carried a small black purse.

The King, though he strode toward the President with a broad smile, his hand extended for a handshake, wore the full-dress uniform of a British admiral: fore-and-aft cocked hat, heavy epaulettes, fourragère, an array of medals, sleeves elaborately embroidered with gold stripes and trefoil, white gloves, trousers with a broad red stripe, and, finally, a formal sword in an elaborate scabbard.

The Queen wore one of the hats she would affect all her life, an ankle-length white dress with a scalloped hem, a white jacket trimmed on the sleeves with fluffy white fur, white gloves, and three strands of large pearls.

Both Roosevelts were much taller than the King and Queen. They discovered immediately that they had to bend over to talk with them.

As the party left Union Station a twenty-one gun salute was fired. Preceded by motorcycles and cars of Secret Service men, the open limousine carrying the President and First Lady and the King and Queen, approached the Capitol on Delaware Avenue, turned onto Constitution Avenue briefly, then onto Pennsylvania Avenue on its way to the White House. The limousine was followed by marching troops and rumbling tanks.

As many as half a million people lined the streets between the station and the White House, cheering wildly and waving American and British flags. Other batteries of artillery cracked out more salutes. The air above the parade route was filled with scores of overflying airplanes.

Mrs. Roosevelt tried at first to point out to the Queen the significance of some of the buildings along the route, but the cheers and salutes made it impossible. Queen Elizabeth raised a silk umbrella to shield herself from the hot Washington sunlight. She reacted warmly to the crowd, smiling, nodding, and waving as the procession moved toward the White House.

When the cars passed through the gates, the crowd pressed to the fence and continued cheering. Mrs. Roosevelt told the Queen it was the warmest welcome she had ever seen Washington give to anyone.

*   *   *

In the White House the royal couple were first escorted to the East Room, where the Washington diplomatic corps was presented to them. After that, they went to the rooms they would occupy during their visit—the Queen in the northeast bedroom suite that would be known after that day as the Queen's Room. Shortly they would come down for a private lunch.

Their coming down for lunch, Mrs. Roosevelt decided, would be a good time for Tommy Thompson, Edith Helm, and Lucinda Robinson—people who had worked hard on the arrangements for the visit—to be presented. She had arranged also for the children of cabinet members to stand along the hall to watch the King and Queen walk by. The President agreed with her that as many of the staff and as many children should see the royal couple as was possible without it becoming obtrusive.

She called Edith Helm and told her to come to the Red Room and bring Lucinda with her.

"I haven't seen Lucinda for the past hour or so," said Edith Helm. "I've no idea where she's gone."

"Probably in the private dining room, overseeing arrangements," suggested the First Lady.

"No. I checked there. And with the kitchen staff, too. I simply don't know where she's got to, and it's an inappropriate time for her to be missing."

"I'm sure she's hard at work somewhere and will turn up."

"I hope so. I do hope so."

No one but the royal couple, Canadian Prime Minister Mackenzie King, two equerries, one lady in waiting, Missy LeHand, and the immediate Roosevelt family had been invited to the private lunch. James, Elliott, and Franklin Jr. were there, with their wives. Heirs to their father's buoyancy and zest, the boys, as their parents called them, often became embroiled in vociferous arguments at the table. Not today. Even they were subdued by the presence of a king and queen—to the point that the President jovially inquired of Elliott if he and his brothers had eaten something that didn't agree with them.

The next event of that full day was a drive around Washington, to show the King and Queen some of the sights. Their route had been announced, and they were once again greeted by cheering crowds. After that, the King and Queen attended a garden party at the British Embassy at tea time.

The Roosevelts did not attend the garden party. The President used the time for a rest. Mrs. Roosevelt, in her office, inquired again after Lucinda Robinson. No one had seen her. The First Lady called the Secret Service office and asked the agents to look for her. She received an answer that the agents were greatly overburdened with the security arrangements for the royal visit and that it would be difficult to spare a man to look for Lucinda Robinson.

"I am concerned," Mrs. Roosevelt remarked to Tommy Thompson. "Lucinda has always been most faithful to her work. I can't imagine where she could have gone, or why."

"With all due respect, I suggest you begin to think about the state dinner this evening."

The state dinner was a gala occasion. The horseshoe-shaped table was set with the best the White House had to offer in china, silver, and crystal. The women wore their finest dresses and every jewel they possessed. The men wore whatever decorations they had. The Queen, wearing a glittering tiara, sat to the President's right. Mrs. John Nance Garner, wife of the Vice President, sat to his left. The First Lady sat between the King and the Vice President. Prime Minister Mackenzie King, members of the Cabinet, ambassadors, generals, and admirals, and their wives, filled the remaining seats.

The President, speaking without the notes he had prepared for the occasion, toasted the King with a five-minute speech.

Musical entertainment had been arranged. Kate Smith sang "When the Moon Comes Over the Mountain," at the King's special request. Marian Anderson—the great black singer who had been refused the stage of Constitution Hall by its owners, the Daughters of the American Revolution— sang some spirituals and then classical numbers. Ordinarily she did not want to sing spirituals, but Mrs. Roosevelt had remarked to her they were perhaps the only true orginally American music. Some folk singers followed.

The President returned to the second floor and the family quarters alone, propelling his wheelchair quickly and confidently with thrusts of his powerful arms. The First Lady accompanied the King and Queen up the grand stairway to their rooms in the east end of the floor.

"I hope we haven't exhausted you," she said to the royal couple. "It has been an extraordinarily long and full day."

"Not at all," said King George. "For us it has been a typical day."

"And a very lovely one," added the Queen.

Before she retired, Mrs. Roosevelt picked up her bedside telephone and told the operator to ring the Secret Service office. She asked the officer on duty if Lucinda Robinson had been located. The officer said he was not aware that she had.

On Friday, the second day of the royal visit, the King and Queen went early in the morning to the British Embassy for a reception. After that they went to the Capitol where they were received by members of the Senate and House of Representatives. The President and First Lady would meet them for lunch aboard the presidential yacht.

Again, Mrs. Roosevelt called the Secret Service office. Gerald Baines, a senior agent, spoke with her and said he would come to her office to give her a full report on the effort to find Lucinda Robinson.

Baines was a florid man, his bald head flecked with liver spots, his modestly rotund belly shoving out the vest of his gray suit. In ordinary circumstances, he was bright and cheerful, ready with a quip, a smile fixed on his shiny face. This morning he was grim.

"I guess yesterday I didn't take the matter of Miss Robinson too seriously," he confessed. "With all the—"

"I know the royal visit has imposed a heavy burden," the First Lady interrupted.

Baines allowed himself a wry smile. He shook his head and said, "The Scotland Yard boys have their own ideas about how things should be done. Anyway, I am sorry to have to tell you that we have not located Miss Robinson. I became really worried about her when I found out she did not go home last night. I telephoned her boardinghouse in the middle of the evening, was told she had not yet come in, and left word for her to call the Secret Service office when she did come in. I called again this morning, and her landlady told me Miss Robinson had not come home all night."

"This is very unlike her," said Mrs. Roosevelt. "She is a responsible young woman."

"I had supposed so," said Baines.

"Well . . . Give the matter as much attention as you can, Mr. Baines."

"I will, Ma'am."

"And send me word if you find her."

The presidential yacht was U.S.S. *Potomac*. The President and First Lady, the King and Queen, and guests ate lunch on the way down the river to Mount Vernon, where the King laid a wreath on the tomb of George Washington. After that the party visited a Civilian Conservation Corps camp where the

King closely inspected everything and asked many questions. He was genuinely interested and explained later that he hoped something similar to the CCC could be established in Great Britain. Before returning to the White House they visited Arlington National Cemetery, where the King laid a wreath on the Tomb of the Unknown Soldier.

"Perhaps," said Mrs. Roosevelt to the Queen as they rode together in the car on the way back to the White House, "you can help me solve a small problem."

"I should be happy to."

"As you have noticed, the children of cabinet officers and others have been assembled in the halls, to see you and the King walk past. One little girl has missed you, however. Her name is Diana Hopkins, the daughter of the President's very good friend Harry Hopkins. She is eight years old. My problem is that little Diana's vision of a queen is that of a woman wearing a crown and perhaps carrying a scepter. I should like to present her, but . . . you see my little problem."

"It is easily solved," said Queen Elizabeth. "Present her as we are leaving for the embassy dinner this evening. I shall be wearing a crown and many jewels and will probably look a little more like what the child expects."

It was done. Diana Hopkins told her father, "Oh, Daddy, I have seen the fairy queen!"

After the dinner at the British Embassy the royal couple boarded a train for New York. The Roosevelts returned briefly to the White House, then boarded POTUS, the presidential train, which left immediately for Hyde Park. Mrs. Roosevelt had time to inquire one more time after Lucinda Robinson. She was told the young woman still had not been found. The District police had been called and had joined the search.

* * *

The King and Queen spent most of Saturday in New York City, as guests of Mayor LaGuardia. The Roosevelts spent Saturday preparing for the royal visit to Hyde Park.

Joined by the President's mother, they waited in the library for the royal party to arrive at the cocktail hour. The President had his cocktail table before him and was ready to mix drinks.

"Franklin," his mother said, "I do not approve of cocktails, as you know. You should offer the King tea."

When the King and Queen arrived, the President offered them cocktails, saying to the King, "I do this with some trepidation. My mother thinks I should offer you tea. She does not approve of cocktails."

"Neither does my mother," said the King, as he accepted a whisky and soda.

On Sunday morning the two families attended church. The rector pointedly remarked that attendance would be much improved if every member of the congregation brought his guests to church the way President Roosevelt did.

Mrs. Roosevelt was personally responsible for only one meal during the royal visit, and that was the picnic lunch served that Sunday afternoon. Although a variety of picnic foods was served, the high point of the picnic came when the King was offered an American delicacy he had never before seen or tasted.

As the King looked skeptically at what was on his paper plate, the President told him, "We call it a hotdog. You might want some mustard."

The King accepted the mustard jar and slid the knife along the wiener. Then, with a pessimistic look, he essayed a bite. "It is good, my dear," he said to the Queen.

"They are excellent," said the Queen.

"They go well with beer," said the President.

The King accepted a glass of beer and drank it. "I say," he asked, "can I have another—er—hot dog?"

Early in the evening the King and Queen boarded a train for their return to Canada, from where they would board a ship and go home. In the morning the President and First Lady boarded POTUS once again.

Back in the White House, on Monday morning Mrs. Roosevelt immediately inquired about Lucinda Robinson. Once again, Gerald Baines said he would come to her office to report.

He was grim. "We found her this morning," he said. "But . . . She is dead. What is more, she has been murdered."

"Murdered? Are you sure?"

Baines nodded. "No question about it. She was strangled with a piece of clothesline rope. The body was found in the big linen closet on the third floor, under a pile of dirty bed-clothes. When a maid went in with a laundry cart this morning, to gather up all those bedclothes and take them down to the laundry, she found the body."

"Oh dear . . ."

"We are almost certain we know who did it."

"Indeed? Who?"

"A young lawyer who works for Mr. Hopkins. David Lasky."

"I know Mr. Lasky. What makes you think he did it?"

"Two things, Ma'am. In the first place, the D.C. police found incriminating letters in Miss Robinson's room. In the second place, David Lasky has absquatulated."

"I guess this letter explains the most," said Captain Ed Kennelly, handing the First Lady a letter. "You can handle it. We've taken the prints off it. They are his and hers."

Captain Kennelly was a tall, craggy, red-faced, white-haired Irishman who spoke with a pronounced brogue. He and Mrs. Roosevelt knew each other very well. They had worked together on a number of earlier investigations and had developed an affectionate mutual respect. Out of deference to her, he had crushed out one of his ever-present Luckies just before she came into his office. Even so, the room still reeked of cigarette smoke, mixed with the sharp odor of cold, stale coffee and the not-unpleasant odor of a cheese Danish going stale on a paper plate. The office was as untidy and dusty as it always was, and as always the First Lady wondered why someone, if not Captain Kennelly himself, did not bother to sweep the dead flies off the windowsill.

She had come to police headquarters, though it was late. Telephoned at home, Kennelly had returned and arrived about the time when she and Baines did. She wore a white dress and a white straw hat. They had entered the building through the rear door she always used when she became involved in a police investigation—avoiding the police reporters who always hung around.

She read the letter. It had been typed on a typewriter badly in need of a change of ribbon, by an unskillful typist who had misstruck many letters and x'ed over them instead of trying to erase and type over. Even with the x'ed-out corrections, many errors remained.

Mr Darling Lucinda,

    It is xxxxxxxxx impossible for me to expr ess to you the depth of my love. I have tried xxxxx every way to tell you . I much doubt that you feel the same way about me but I beg you to xxx consider what I offer you—*un dying dvotion*. I have to say somthing about the Krxt. He is an *evil* man! You know what I mean. You m ust not let the Kraut come btween us.

Lucxda I would rather *we both died* than for you to
fall into the dirty hands of that man. I mean that. Do
not betrx me. I wont stand for that.

Best love
DAVE

"We have no idea who 'the Kraut' is," said Kennelly. "Look
at this letter, though."

She read a second one, this handwritten in blue ink. Two
sentences read, "Don't think you can leave me for that man. I
would kill both of you before I would allow that."

"How do you know Mr. Lasky is not dead as well?" asked
Mrs. Roosevelt.

"We don't. Every police department on the East Coast has
been alerted to look for him—particularly in Florida, which
is where he is from."

"I last saw Lucinda on Thursday morning, shortly before
the President and I left for Union Station. Did anyone see her
later?"

Baines answered. "Obviously, you were not the last person
who saw her alive," he said. "But no one remembers seeing
her after midmorning. Sometime, probably around eleven
o'clock, Lucinda Robinson disappeared."

"Why would she have been on the third floor?" asked the
First Lady.

"No one knows," said Baines. "Also, no one remembers
seeing her going up there."

"No one would, necessarily," said Mrs. Roosevelt. "*I* can
move from one floor to another in the White House, using the
private elevators and the various stairs, and not be seen."

"The body had to be moved," said Baines. "Lucinda Robinson may have had reason to be on the third floor but not in
the linen closet."

"It was a very busy time," said Mrs. Roosevelt. "People

were moving all over, preparing for the royal visit. I don't see how anyone could have carried a dead body very far without being observed."

"A good point," said Kennelly.

"Then, as to Mr. Lasky . . . When did *he* disappear?"

"He was here Friday morning, for sure," said Baines. "People saw him. No one remembers seeing him after noon. Mr. Hopkins's staff say he was in the office in the morning but they never saw him after noon."

Mrs. Roosevelt frowned. "Is that not an odd circumstance?" she asked. "If he murdered Lucinda Robinson Thursday morning and then fled . . . disappeared, why would he come to work in the White House twenty-four hours after the murder and only *then* flee?"

"Maybe," said Kennelly, "he thought he'd hidden the body so well it would not be found for several days."

"In the linen closet? With all the activity of setting up rooms for the many members of the royal party? On Thursday, maids must have visited that closet many times."

"We have further questions to ask," said Baines.

Mrs. Roosevelt drew a deep breath. "I am afraid I must ask to be shown the body, Captain Kennelly."

Kennelly had learned by now that there was no point in protesting to the First Lady that a dead body in the morgue was something she should not see. And so, though it was approaching midnight, he arranged a clandestine visit by the wife of the President of the United States to the District morgue.

"She won't be here after tomorrow morning," said the morgue attendant, a young man in white. "Her parents have applied for the body and will take it home to Minnesota for burial. In fact, they don't like the fact that it's here at all. They want it moved to a funeral home and laid out. They're on a train now, on their way here."

He opened a door, pulled out a drawer, lifted off a sheet, and the naked body of Lucinda Robinson lay exposed in harsh light.

She had been pale. Dead for more than seventy-two hours, she was pallid and stiff. The rope that had been used to strangle her had left a vivid bruise, now almost black, around her throat. Her face was distorted. She was hardly recognizable, and Mrs. Roosevelt reflected that it *would* be well if she could be delivered to an undertaker so that he could work on her before her parents saw her—though it was doubtful that even the most artful undertaker could restore any semblance of her appearance in life. Even so, the First Lady quietly suggested to Kennelly that the body be released as soon as possible.

"No autopsy was done," said Kennelly. "It's obvious what killed her. The coroner went over every inch of her, though. There are no bruises. We have to think the killer caught her from behind, threw the rope over her head, and strangled her—without hitting her or anything. Notice the abrasions on her throat. Traces of skin were found under her fingernails. She clawed at the rope, trying to pull it loose."

"Ghastly!" Mrs. Roosevelt shuddered.

"I'm afraid that's about all there is to learn from the body," said Kennelly.

"Are we certain she was not raped?"

"Yes, Ma'am. She was examined for that. She was not raped."

The First Lady opened her purse and pulled out a mechanical pencil. She used it to point at a small mark in the right armpit. "Have you identified that?" she asked.

Kennelly bent over the body and frowned at the mark. He shook his head. "We noticed it, I think, but didn't attach any significance to it. It's not the kind of mark that has anything to do with killing anybody."

"I suppose," said Mrs. Roosevelt, "I risk looking like Sherlock Holmes if I ask for a magnifying glass, but if someone has one—"

The young attendant hurried away and returned in a moment with a big round magnifying glass. The First Lady took it and stared intently through it at the small mark in the armpit. Then she moved around and examined a similar mark in the left armpit.

"An abrasion," she said. "Not a bruise. But almost identical marks in each armpit. The skin has been disturbed, a little rubbed off. What could have caused that? What could she have been doing that would make marks like that in her armpits? Can we turn her over, gentlemen?"

Kennelly helped the attendant roll the stiff corpse over on its face.

The same small marks appeared on both armpits at the back. In fact, the marks ran all the way through the body's armpits, though they were much less distinct inside the armpits.

"Does anyone but me find these marks curious?" asked Mrs. Roosevelt. "The skin seems to have been rather firmly scraped—enough to break the skin—and yet there are no bruises. Uh . . . where are her clothes?"

The clothes were in a brown paper bag. The body was covered with its sheet and rolled back into its little vault, and the clothes were laid out on the autopsy table: the white linen dress with pattern of tiny violet flowers and green leaves, the white patent-leather belt that had cinched it at the waist, a slip, a white brassiere, white panties, a white garter belt, all of silk, stockings, and a pair of white shoes.

"What is this stain?" asked Mrs. Roosevelt, looking at a yellow stain on the skirt.

"Urine," said Kennelly. "When a person dies, the muscles that hold back urine relax. The panties are stained the same way."

Mrs. Roosevelt grimaced. "I wish I hadn't asked," she said.

"Sometimes the bowels, too," said Kennelly.

Mrs. Roosevelt frowned and turned her attention to something else. "Unless I am mistaken," she said, "I am looking at marks in the armpits of this dress that correspond to the marks in the armpits of the body. Notice how the fabric has been scraped at the corresponding places."

Kennelly squinted at the dress. What Mrs. Roosevelt said was true. The fabric had, at the very least, been subjected to some sort of stress at the armpits.

"Now I'm going to make a suggestion," she continued. "If you have the *inside* of the armpits of this dress examined under a microscope, I predict you will find lots of skin cells in the weave."

"I wouldn't be surprised," Kennelly muttered, "if you have an explanation for what we overlooked—and you haven't."

"A possible explanation," she said. "After Lucinda was dead, her murderer looped a rope around her, under her armpits, and used it to move her from one place to another. Since there are no abrasions on her bottom or on her hips, I guess she wasn't dragged through the halls. The condition of this dress argues that, too. She was lifted, I should think. Up an elevator shaft or stairwell."

"The rope that strangled her caused dark bruises," said Baines. "Why didn't the rope under her armpits do the same?"

"I will ask Captain Kennelly to check with the coroner about that. I believe I read somewhere that once a body has been dead a certain length of time, it no long bruises. A bruise is, after all, blood—blood outside a vessel ruptured by a trauma. Once it is no longer circulating and has in fact coagulated . . . I think the coroner will confirm this."

"I don't have to ask the coroner. It's true," said Kennelly.

"Very well, then," said Mrs. Roosevelt. "Lucinda Robinson was probably killed Thursday morning. She was hidden somewhere, then moved up to the linen closet later."

"And so much later," Kennelly added, "that her body no longer bruised."

Mrs. Roosevelt nodded and allowed a flicker of a smile to cross her face. "We know so much," she said, "and yet so little. Is Mr. Lasky alive? If so, where is he? Who is 'the Kraut'? *Why* was Lucinda killed? What was the motive?"

Ed Kennelly smiled wryly. "When you get into a case, it's never simple," he said. "Starts out simple, but—"

"I'm sorry," she interrupted.

"Don't be," he said firmly. "You've stopped me from doing some dumb things, and I'm one hundred per cent grateful."

On Tuesday morning Mrs. Roosevelt dictated two "My Day" columns. She was syndicated in nearly one hundred newspapers across the country. Each column, typically about six hundred words long, was an account of her day in the White House or of her travels.

This morning she chose to tell what her mother-in-law would shortly complain was a family secret that should never have been revealed to the public—first, that at Hyde Park a serving table had collapsed during the dinner for the King and Queen, shattering dishes and scattering food on the dining room floor, and, second, that a butler had tripped carrying a tray of drinks to the library after dinner, and bottles, glasses, ice, and water had fallen to the floor in a great crash. The King and Queen, the First Lady wrote, had seemed not to notice.

Then, about 9:30, she went to the third floor to look at the linen closet where the body of Lucinda Robinson had been found. She was accompanied by Agent Gerald Baines.

The large closet had, of course, been entirely tidied up.

Linens and blankets, towels and washcloths filled the shelves in tidy ranks. The room offered no clue as to how the body had been brought there, much less as to who had killed the young woman and why.

The maid who had found the corpse had been called to join the First Lady on the third floor. She arrived while Mrs. Roosevelt and Baines stood outside the closet, talking quietly.

Her name was Carolyn Flowers. She was a Negro girl. Mrs. Roosevelt guessed she was no more than twenty years old. She was exceptionally attractive, with a flawless complexion, chocolate-colored, a flat little nose, and perfect white teeth. She wore a gray dress with a white starched apron.

Mrs. Roosevelt tried to put the girl at ease. She smiled at her and said, "So you found the body in the closet?"

"Yes, Ma'am, Ah did," said Carolyn. She spoke with the accent common to the District natives. "Ah found her right there."

"Under a pile of dirty linen. Was that a big pile?"

"Yes, Ma'am. Unusual big pile. We made beds and put out towels for the King and the Queen and all them visitors, on Wednesday. Then they all came on Thursday and slep' in the beds that night, and Friday mornin' we tore all the beds apart and made 'em up fresh. That made a *big* pile of sheets and stuff. Couldn't 'xactly call it dirty, only slep' on one night. Anyway, they mos' all left on Friday and didn't sleep in those beds Friday night. Even so, we tore 'em all apart Saturday morning. Made the pile twicet as big!"

"So, there wasn't a big pile of laundry on the floor of that linen closet until Friday morning?"

"No, Ma'am, not till Friday morning."

"And not even then, until after the guests were out of their rooms and you could strip the beds."

"That's right."

"When you first came into this closet on Friday morning, the body could not have been here. Is that right?"

The maid nodded. "First time I looked in here, there was maybe a coupla sheets, maybe a few towels on the floor. Couldn't have been no body. Wasn't enough stuff to cover it so's you wouldn't notice it."

"When you stripped the beds again on Saturday morning and brought the sheets and things up here, was the pile already so big it could have covered the body?"

"Yes, Ma'am. I been thinkin' 'bout that. Maybe when we wuz pilin' stuff in here Saturday morning, we were coverin' a *corpse!* Deeper 'n deeper!"

"All of this laundry accumulated here and was not taken down to be washed until yesterday morning," said Mrs. Roosevelt. "Why was that?"

The girl's eyes widened. "Why . . . Miz Roosevelt, *Monday is wash day!*"

The First Lady smiled. "Of course," she said. She remembered it was a custom, "since the memory of man runneth not to the contrary" in the old Blackstonian cliché, that in every well run household clothes were washed on Monday and ironed on Tuesday.

Baines spoke. "All right, Carolyn. The body was not here on Friday morning, but it could have been here on Saturday morning. Is that what you're telling us?"

"Yes, suh. It was not here Friday morning, for sure. Not when we first came in. Then after we piled a big heap up, it could have been."

Mrs. Roosevelt closed the door of the linen closet and walked out into the central corridor of the third floor. The guests rooms there were not grand. Members of the royal party's staff had occupied these rooms during the visit. The dignitaries, except the King and Queen, had stayed at the British Embassy. Missy LeHand had a modest suite, bedroom and sitting room, up here. Louis McHenry Howe had a suite up here, while he lived. Harry Hopkins lived on the third floor from time to time.

A broad corridor crossed the third floor east to west. A much narrower corridor crossed north to south. Besides the bedrooms and sitting rooms, the third floor had a storage area, with a large cedar closet for woolens and eight other storage rooms besides the linen closet.

Doors led out to the roof, where a broad promenade circled the entire floor. A glassed-in sunroom stood above the south portico and the oval rooms below.

Access to the third floor was provided by several sets of stairs and the two elevators that reached all the floors.

"I am most curious as to how the body was moved to the third floor," said Mrs. Roosevelt. "You work up here, Carolyn, and probably know as much about the house as anyone. Can you think of any way the body could have been brought up from one of the lower floors without anyone seeing?"

"No, Ma'am."

"It could hardly have been carried up the stairs, I should think. Nor brought up on an elevator, either. Are there air shafts, Mr. Baines?"

Baines shook his head.

"Well . . . Well, thank you, Carolyn. You have been most helpful."

Mrs. Roosevelt and Baines went to the East Wing. Edith Helm met them at the door of the social secretary's office. Lucinda Robinson's desk was just outside that office. Her desk had been cleared of all papers. A vase containing a spray of gladiolas sat in the middle of the desk.

"I can't believe she was killed in the East Wing," said Mrs. Helm. "This was a very busy place on Thursday morning.

Anyway, where could the body have been hidden? If it were moved from here, it would have had to be carried through the arcade." She shook her head. "I think Lucinda left here for some reason and met her death in the White House itself. Or on the grounds."

"I should like to ask," said Mrs. Roosevelt, "if you observed a relationship between Lucinda and David Lasky."

"Yes, I did," said Mrs. Helm. "He came over here to visit her from time to time. He was a very respectful, courteous young man, and he never stayed more than a minute. He never interrupted her work for more than a minute."

"Did any other men come to see her?"

Mrs. Helm shook her head. "None . . . except someone on business."

"Have you heard anyone referred to as 'the Kraut'? Do you have any idea who might be meant by that term?"

"No," said Mrs. Helm.

"Would you guess that Lucinda was in love with Mr. Lasky?"

Mrs. Helm smiled sympathetically. "I thought he was smitten with her. He sent her flowers now and again. I don't think she was smitten with him. I suspect that what he wrote on the cards with the flowers embarrassed her."

"Have you searched her desk?" Mrs. Roosevelt asked Gerald Baines.

"Yes, Ma'am. We didn't find anything in particular."

"Do you mind if I look?"

The First Lady opened the center drawer of the small yellow-oak desk. It contained an assortment of the usual things found in desk drawers: paper clips, pencils, a bottle of ink, a nail file, a bottle of aspirin tablets, and so on.

She noticed a card lying under a box of paper clips and picked it up. It was the kind of foldover card that often came with flowers, and she wondered if this was one that had embarrassed Lucinda Robinson. She read it—

Herzliche Glückwünsche !

Lassen Sie von sich hören.

K

" 'Best wishes. Let me hear from you,' " Mrs. Roosevelt translated. "And it would seem likely that 'K' is 'the Kraut' that Mr. Lasky complained of. It's interesting, isn't it, that she saved this card and none of the others. I wonder if there are fingerprints on it, Mr. Baines."

"Let's put it in an envelope and ask Kennelly to find out," said Baines.

"I wonder," said Mrs. Roosevelt, as she and Baines walked back through the arcade and into the first floor of the White House, "if something like that card was not overlooked by the District police officers who searched Lucinda's room."

"I believe you are telling me you would like to go there," said Baines dryly.

In Captain Kennelly's car on the way to the boardinghouse where Lucinda Robinson had lived, the First Lady changed into something of a disguise. She had donned a severe dark-blue suit, and now she covered her hair with a dark-blue turban. She wore sunglasses. To complete the disguise, Kennelly pinned a D.C. detective's badge on her breast pocket. She added to it further by reddening her lips with lipstick.

The boardinghouse was owned and run by an elderly couple. The gray-haired woman was tearful as she spoke of

Lucinda. Her husband led the First Lady, Kennelly, and Baines to the second-floor room Lucinda had rented.

It was typical of the rooms government girls rented in Washington: a large, sunny bedroom on the front of the house, furnished with a four-poster double bed, an easy chair upholstered in worn rose-colored plush, a writing table with straight chair, a dresser on which sat a large white bowl and pitcher. The bathroom was down the hall. A chamber pot sat almost out of sight under the bed, and Mrs. Roosevelt wondered if Lucinda had ever used it, or had ever washed at the bowl with water carried in in the pitcher.

The question of whether or not Lucinda ever used the pitcher and bowl was quickly answered when Mrs. Roosevelt looked in the bowl and saw a red rubber douche syringe.

"Only complaint I ever had about her," said the landlord, who had followed them into the room. "She poured the water out the window."

Kennelly thanked the man and gently asked him to leave them alone. "You know how police work is," he said.

The man nodded sagely, as if he did know, intimately, and closed the door as he left.

Mrs. Roosevelt looked at the clothes hanging in the closet. "A very nice wardrobe," she remarked. "When she went out in the evening, she was handsomely dressed."

"Compensation for not having been an exceptionally beautiful girl," said Kennelly.

The underwear in the dresser drawers was all silk, some of it trimmed with lace.

In the top drawer of the dresser there was another card signed "K." It read—

Lassen Sie nun fief förmn fo sfunle nain möglif.

" 'Let me hear from you as soon as possible.' K seems to have suffered from an anxiety about not hearing from Lucinda as often or as soon as he wished," said Mrs. Roosevelt. "Let's take this card for fingerprints as well."

"I didn't figure there was anything significant about *this*," said Kennelly, pointing to a small book lying on the writing table. *Sexual Feeling in Woman* by Dr. G. Lombard Kelly. "Normal curiosity, I supposed."

Mrs. Roosevelt nodded. "Many young women, away from their homes and alone for the first time, feel such a curiosity."

She continued to look through the contents of the room and its closet. Hanging in the closet was a beaded evening bag. The First Lady opened it and looked inside. It contained the usual things for such a bag: a lipstick, a handkerchief, a compact, a package of Spuds cigarettes, and a Zippo lighter. Also a small package—

RAMSES
RUBBER PROPHYLACTICS
Form-fitting. Super-thin.
<u>SOLD FOR PREVENTION OF DISEASE ONLY.</u>

"It looks as if our tragic little victim was not an innocent little girl," said Kennelly.

"I do not think that necessarily follows from this discovery," said Mrs. Roosevelt.

"But the investigation takes a new turn," said Kennelly. "I'd like to know if Mr. David Lasky is still alive."

"Would it be inappropriate," asked Mrs. Roosevelt, "if we took a look at *his* living quarters? After all, I *am* already wearing this ludicrous disguise."

At the three-story brick apartment building where David Lasky had lived on Eye Street, Ed Kennelly introduced the First Lady to the bemused receptionist as "Detective Broderick." They went up to the apartment, and it was immediately apparent that Lasky had lived in some style, in more style in fact than his salary as a young government lawyer could have sustained.

The apartment had a living room, a small dining room, a bedroom, kitchen, and bath. It was rented furnished, as was Lucinda's room; but the furniture was handsome, reproductions of the Colonial-style pieces found in some of the better Georgetown houses. The color motif was green: ivory walls and ceilings above a silver-green wainscoting and dark green rugs on a parquet floor. Clustered on a wall above the dining table were Lasky's diplomas. He was a graduate of Princeton and of Harvard Law, and he was admitted to the practice of his profession in Florida and New York, as well as in the various federal courts and the District of Columbia.

He had a big Zenith floor-model radio, equipped to bring in shortwave broadcasts from all over the world. Though he had no bookshelves, books were stacked everywhere: on tables, on top of the radio, even some on the floor. He seemed to be an avid reader of history and biography, and Mrs. Roosevelt noted that some of the books were in German and some in French.

"People's private things tend to be found in their bedrooms," she said.

Lasky's bed was neatly made, perhaps by a housemaid. His well pressed suits were hung in his closet. Shirts and underwear filled his bureau drawers.

"He left suddenly," said Kennelly.

"Or maybe was murdered, too," said Mrs. Roosevelt.

"Maybe. But notice, there's no suitcase in the closet. Maybe he didn't have one. Notice also the stack of laundered shirts. See the empty space beside it? That suggests to me that he took three or four other shirts when he went. Same way with the underwear and socks. The way that stuff is stacked in the drawers, it looks like he grabbed some out."

"He seems to have had a penchant for neatness," said the First Lady, frowning over a drawer. "Doesn't the receptionist know when he left?"

"No. Tenants can go out the back. Anyway, no one who lives here has to check in and out or anything like that. He could have walked past her desk while she was carrying the mail around or picking up a cup of coffee."

A picture of Lucinda Robinson, in a silver frame, sat on the night table beside the bed. "She never looked that beautiful," said Baines dryly.

She was not wearing her spectacles in the photograph. Her hair was lighted from behind, creating a sort of halo around her head. As photographed by some highly skilled photographer, Lucinda looked like a puffier Jean Harlow.

She had autographed the picture. "Okay, Davy. Is this what you wanted? Your affectionate friend, Lucy."

"That's hardly a declaration of undying love," said Baines. From any evidence in the apartment, Lasky did not smoke. Mrs. Roosevelt suggested they take with them a collection of a dozen or so matchbooks from the top bureau drawer. They were from restaurants and nightclubs in the Washington area.

"Dolly's . . ." Kennelly mused, reading from a matchbook. "That's quite a joint. Over in Virginia. If our boy was a member of Dolly's—and you have to be a member to get in—he was no innocent, either."

"Little things," said Mrs. Roosevelt.

"I get your point," said Kennelly. "I didn't search this place myself. A coupla younger guys did it."

"Did they lift the rugs to see if anything was hidden under them?" asked the First Lady.

Kennelly shrugged. "I suppose so."

"Shall we find out?"

When they lifted one of the rugs in the living room, the first thing they found was David Lasky's passport.

"Damn!" Kennelly complained. "They *didn't* look under the rugs."

Next they found five hundred dollars in cash.

"It is difficult to believe a man fled from arrest and left behind his passport and this much money," said Mrs. Roosevelt.

"Everything we see raises more questions," said Kennelly.

"In fact," said the First Lady, "so far as I can see, there is only one certainty in this case, only one fact established beyond dispute."

"And what is that?" asked Gerald Baines.

"That Lucinda Robinson is dead."

Still in the guise of Detective Broderick, the First Lady returned to District police headquarters with Captain Kennelly. She went there because she wanted to hear the results of the fingerprint examination of the card she had found in Lucinda's desk drawer earlier in the day.

"There's a man waiting to see you, Captain," a uniformed sergeant told Kennelly. "He's been waiting quite a while."

"He'll have to wait a little longer," said Kennelly.

"He says he needs to talk to you about the murder of Lucinda Robinson."

"Well," said Mrs. Roosevelt. "Perhaps . . ."

In minutes she and Baines sat in a darkened room, facing the back side of a two-way mirror. Ed Kennelly talked with the young man in a lighted conference room.

"You say your name is . . . ?"

"Robert Grant," said the young man. "I thought you might be looking for me, so—"

"Why would we be looking for you?"

"I read in the paper that Lucinda Robinson is dead, that she was murdered. Since she and I were . . . friends, I thought you might want to see me."

"Friends?"

"Well . . . Intimate friends."

Robert Grant was a tall, handsome, blond man, with thick and unruly light hair, a cleft chin, a ready smile, and an air of self-confidence. He wore a light-blue summer-weight suit with white buttons, a white shirt, and a red satin necktie. His brown-and-white shoes contributed to Kennelly's impression that the young man was rather flashy—to use the term that came to the captain's mind. He lit a Camel and blew the smoke away from Kennelly.

"You didn't come in here to confess, I suppose," said Kennelly dryly.

"Absolutely not," said Grant. "The newspapers say her body was found in the White House. I've never been in the White House. The stories don't say how she was killed. How *was* she killed, Captain? Can you tell me?"

"She was strangled," said Kennelly.

The young man winced. "Oh, God! What an awful way—"

"Mr. Grant . . . Bob, right? Bob, just how close a friend were you of Lucinda Robinson?"

"Do you want the whole story? I had nothing to do with somebody killing her, Captain. I'll take a lie-detector test on that. But a lot of people have seen us together, and more than a few know we slept together—which is why I supposed you might want to talk to me."

"Yeah, I want the whole story," said Kennelly, nodding as he lit a Lucky.

"Okay. I sell automobiles for a living. Chevrolets. I'm a Washingtonian born and bred, and like most fellows my age—I'm twenty-seven—I've watched a lot of government girls come to Washington since the New Deal came in and the agencies expanded. You know, they come in from all over, and it's easy for a fellow to get a date in this town. Lucy—Lucinda—arrived from Minnesota about a year ago. At first she lived in the Bismarck Hotel for Women, and that's where I met her. Fellows go over there and hang around the lobby to meet the new girls."

"So I've heard," said Kennelly.

"Having a car to drive is an advantage," said Grant. "Anyway, I met Lucy. I suppose you've seen her . . . Or—"

"I've seen her body."

"Yeah . . . Well, you could see she wasn't the world's prettiest girl. I probably wouldn't have asked her to go out with me, but another fellow who didn't have a car asked me to take him and his date to a roadhouse in Maryland to dance, and— I'd need a date, too, and his date asked Lucy before I could interrupt. Well, in the course of that evening, I learned a lot of things about Lucy and got a very different idea about her."

"Like what?" Kennelly asked.

"Well . . . To start with, Lucy was very well educated. She

had a college degree from some college in Minnesota. She could speak German and some French. She loved working at the White House, thought it was the greatest thing in the world to have got in there; but what she really wanted to do was get into the diplomatic service some way. With her German, she hoped she could get assigned to the embassy in Berlin. Or maybe she could get a job in the German embassy here."

"My word," Mrs. Roosevelt whispered to Baines in the room beyond the mirror. "Didn't the girl realize the character of the present German régime?"

"Besides," Grant went on, "she was pretty naive. When she came to Washington, it was the first time she was ever away from home. You see, that college she went to—uh, Saint Olaf, I think it's called—is in her home town. Her father's a professor there."

"Whatta you mean by naive?" Kennelly asked. *"How* was she naive?"

The young man took a long, thoughtful puff on his cigarette and put it aside in the ashtray on the table. "Let's put it this way. She was very, very affectionate. It was like she'd never been kissed before. And she *wanted* to be kissed! That first evening I was with her, things went pretty far between us. Not all the way, but . . . pretty far. It was like she wanted to make up for lost time."

"So, before long things did go all the way, I suppose," said Kennelly in a police-wry tone.

Grant shrugged. "She was free, white, and twenty-one," he said. "She was twenty-two, actually."

"Where did this intimacy take place?"

"Once in the car. After that, in my rooms."

"May I draw the curtain of modesty over this, or is there something more about it you need to tell me?" asked Kennelly.

"Only that she took to it like a duck to water. If she'd never done it before, she sure knew how!"

Kennelly glanced at the mirror. Apparently he could not resist glancing toward the First Lady, who was back there witnessing and hearing it all. "Bob . . ." he said. "When did you meet her?"

"I think it may have been July. July, 1938."

"When did you last see her?"

"Maybe a month ago. About a month ago."

"Had you stopped . . . having intimate relations with her? If so, when did you stop?"

"By . . . December, I think. Never after Christmas."

"Why did you stop?"

"Lucy was not the innocent kid I thought she was. Or maybe she had been and grew up real fast. Let's suppose it was the latter. Once she learned how to catch a man, a car salesman wasn't good enough for her."

"You mean she dumped you for somebody else?"

"Yeah. Yeah. It doesn't do a fellow's ego much good to know that's what happened, does it? I guess I thought I'd introduced an innocent country girl to the . . . You know to what. I guess she introduced me to something."

"Do you recognize the name David Lasky?"

"Sure. You bet."

"She leave you for Lasky?"

"For Lasky? Hardly. But for Lasky and three or four others. I saw her with them—in bars."

"What do you know about Lasky?"

Grant took a moment to light another cigarette. "Money," he said. "Lasky's a lawyer and makes good money. Works at the White House, which is how she met him. But he inherited money, too. He could afford to take her where I couldn't. I thought I was doin' okay to take her around in my own car. Hell, he took her around in cabs. I couldn't compete with that."

"And why should you?" Kennelly asked. "Huh? Why should you? A girl like that—"

Behind the mirror, Mrs. Roosevelt frowned at Baines and wondered what Captain Kennelly was driving at.

"Right," Grant immediately agreed. "After all, every girl in the world has got what she had. Hey. Don't get me wrong. I'd of thought myself lucky to make a permanent connection with a girl like that, even if she wasn't a raving beauty and you sort of slid off to back tables when you took her someplace."

"Let's get back to Lasky," said Kennelly. "He's missing."

"Lasky? Since when?"

"Since the day after Lucinda Robinson died."

Grant shook his head and drew so deeply on his cigarette that he burned a quarter of it in one puff. He continued shaking his head as thick white smoke trickled from his nose and mouth. "If you think *he* killed her, I think you've got it wrong. Hey. If you think he did, that puts *me* a little farther away from it. But— Did you ever see Lasky? Talk to him? You . . . Lucy told me. It was a joke with her, and she told me he was awful well equipped as a man. That says somethin' about Lucy, doesn't it: that she'd tell me a thing like that? But she did. Anyway, except for that maybe, he was a *shrimp!* You ever hear the expression, 'Hat, where'd you get that man?' That's Lasky. He was hid under his hat. Little guy. Shrimp. It had to be his money she went for."

"All right. What about a German? Did she see a German?"

Grant shrugged. "She *spoke* German. But I don't remember ever seeing her with a German man."

Kennelly nodded. "Do you know a club over in Virginia called Dolly's?"

"I've heard of it. Too rich for my blood."

"Okay. You came in and asked to talk. Is there anything else you want to tell me?"

"I came in 'cause I had to figure a guy who'd known Lucy

as well as I did and had been seen with her as much as I had, had to be some kind of suspect. I don't know when she was killed, exactly. You tell me, and I'll tell you where I was at the time."

"Thursday morning," said Kennelly.

"I was on the floor at the agency, tryin' to sell a car or two. I can name guys who'll confirm that."

Kennelly sighed. "Write down your name and address, business address, and both telephone numbers. I'll call you if I need to talk to you."

The fingerprint examination of the card taken from Lucinda Robinson's desk drawer and inscribed in German carried two sets of fingerprints: those of Lucinda and those of the First Lady.

"Now, that is a very curious circumstance, don't you think?" asked Mrs. Roosevelt. "Why are there no fingerprints from the man who wrote on the card?"

"He was wearing gloves," said Baines.

"*Writing* with gloves on?" she asked.

"Well, let's see what we find on the other card, the one we took from her room," said Kennelly.

"If there are none but hers and mine on that," said Mrs. Roosevelt, "then the question grows very interesting indeed."

At seven that evening, the First Lady spoke at a dinner held by the American Booksellers Association. She spoke first in appreciation, since the association was presenting the White House with a gift of one hundred recently published books for its library—most, but not all, American works. She did not have time to look through all the books being given to the White House for its permanent library, but she noticed that among the titles were William Faulkner's *Absalom, Absa-*

lom! and his recent novel, *The Wild Palms;* James T. Farrell's *Studs Lonigan;* Ernest Hemingway's *To Have and to Have Not;* Thomas Wolfe's *Of Time and the River;* T. S. Eliot's *Old Possum's Book of Practical Cats;* James Joyce's *Finnegans Wake;* Charles and Mary Beard's *America in Midpassage;* Van Wyck Brooks's *The Flowering of New England;* Pearl Buck's *The Good Earth;* and Margaret Mitchell's *Gone With the Wind.*

Having effusively thanked the Association for its gift, Mrs. Roosevelt lightened the occasion by telling the assembled authors, agents, and publishers two of the stories of the royal visit that she had already written in her column.

"You see, my mother-in-law lives in rather modest circumstances, though in a fine big house, and does not have staff enough to serve on a grand occasion. For that reason, some of the White House people accompanied us on the train to Hyde Park, to help with the serving of the dinner for royalty. Indeed, they more than helped, because when my mother-in-law's English butler was informed that most of the serving would be done by the White House staff, he elected to take his vacation at that time.

"The White House staff could not have been aware of an eccentricity of one of the serving tables: that is, that one of its legs has been often repaired and is in consequence weak. Never guessing this, the White House people piled it high with heavy dishes. It became overburdened and simply collapsed, sending dishes and food scattering on the floor.

"One of the President's cousins had been kind enough to lend us some china for the royal dinner. In the silence that followed the crash, she spoke out and said, 'I certainly hope the broken china was none of that which *I* lent.' His Majesty King George and Her Majesty Queen Elizabeth simply pretended not to have noticed the crash or overheard the comment.

"They are most gracious people and perfect guests. That which went well, they appreciated. That which did not, they overlooked.

"Their capacity to overlook was surely strained an hour or so later when a butler entering the library with a huge tray of after-dinner drinks omitted to notice that you must descend two steps to enter that room and so fell, making a crash more spectacular than that which followed the collapse of the serving table. So far as I could detect, the King and Queen did not so much as glance toward the source of the clatter. They were talking with my husband and his mother and did not miss a word."

After dinner several authors were brought forward to chat with the First Lady.

Among them was Ernest Hemingway, a young man with a clipped dark mustache and a broad, toothy smile.

"I've read two or three of your books, Mr. Hemingway," she said.

"I've read one of yours, Mrs. Roosevelt," he said.

"I understand your next novel will be about the civil war in Spain," she said. "What will it be called, have you decided yet?"

"I want to call it *For Whom the Bell Tolls.*"

" 'For whom—?' A quotation from—?"

"John Donne. 'Any man's death diminishes me, for I am involved in mankind. And therefore never send to know for whom the bell tolls. It tolls for thee.' "

Mrs. Roosevelt nodded thoughtfully. "Yes . . . I remember now. 'No man is an island entire of itself . . .' "

" 'Every man is a piece of the continent, a part of the main,' " Hemingway continued.

"Oh, yes. Yes, Mr. Hemingway. That is very good, a very apt quotation for our times."

"Have you met Bill Faulkner?" Hemingway asked, nodding

toward a rather vacant-looking dishevelled man who was approaching them.

"I don't believe I've had the honor," she said.

Hemingway introduced them. William Faulkner squinted at her and blinked. "Shuh pleasure," he muttered. He was very drunk. "Give my best wishes . . . to the Pres . . . dunt."

"I shall," said Mrs. Roosevelt.

"Excuse me," said Faulkner as he wandered off.

"It's an illness," said Hemingway. "He's being treated for it. But he has his bad days."

When she left the dinner, she found Gerald Baines waiting for her beside the limousine.

"The Robinson family is at the funeral home," he said somberly. "I thought you'd want to know."

Mrs. Roosevelt nodded. "I must go there."

Lucinda Robinson was laid out in a gray steel, satin-lined casket. She had been dressed in a violet dress, makeup had been used to cover the marks of the rope that had strangled her, and her cheeks and lips had been colored pink. The undertaker had not put her glasses on her closed eyes but had put them in her hands which were folded on her breast.

Professor Robinson was a big man: tall and thickset, with graying dark hair, cut very short. He stood stiff and stern, watching with a critical eye the very few people who arrived to view his daughter. Mrs. Robinson was short and stout. She sat in a corner and sobbed into a handkerchief.

"You do us great honor, Mrs. Roosevelt," said the professor. "I had no idea you would come in person."

"My husband would be with me," she said, "except that you know how difficult it is for him to get about."

"It is very kind of you," he said. "Only four or five people have come."

"Very few people know she's here, Professor Robinson. Many would come if they knew. When will you be leaving?"

"Early tomorrow."

"If you could keep her here another day, I am sure many would come from the White House. Lucinda was very well regarded there."

The professor shook his head. "I must take her home."

"I understand. I really cannot adequately express my sympathy," said Mrs. Roosevelt.

"Mrs. Helm came," said the professor. "It was kind of her. Lucinda wrote us that Mrs. Helm had been generous toward her. Indeed, she wrote of you, saying now nice you had been to her."

"Did Lucinda write often?"

"Twice a week. She described a marvelous life here in Washington. We supposed everything was going well for her."

"I would have supposed so," said Mrs. Roosevelt. "She was very good at her work. She seemed happy and enthusiastic. But, tell me, did she say anything in her letters about a boy-friend?"

"She said she was dating. She didn't mention any young man by name. Is there suspicion that—?"

"Whenever a young woman is murdered, Professor Robinson, any young man she has been seeing is a suspect. Automatically."

"A police captain stopped by. Named . . . uh—"

"Kennelly."

"Yes, Captain Kennelly. I tried to find out if the police have suspects. He was very mysterious."

"That is because he hasn't broken the case, Professor. He has one suspect, but I'm afraid the evidence against that suspect is most inconclusive."

"Well, he assured me on one point," said Professor Robinson sadly. "She had not been . . . abused."

"No, she had not. I asked that question, too."

"That comforted her mother a little."

Mrs. Roosevelt stepped over to the weeping little woman. "My deepest sympathy, Mrs. Robinson," she said quietly.

"Oh, Mrs. Roosevelt! I can't believe . . ."

"We all loved her," said the First Lady simply. "Everyone here did."

"Except one," said the professor grimly.

"I imagine," said Mrs. Roosevelt, "you have reviewed her letters, looking for any suggestion of the motive."

"We read some of them," said Mrs. Robinson. "She wrote about the people she met. She thought she was going to see the King and Queen of England. I . . . don't suppose . . ."

Mrs. Roosevelt lied. "She met them. She had done so much to prepare for their visit."

"And you and the President and so many famous people," whispered Mrs. Robinson, shaking her head.

"What happened to her happened quite suddenly," said Mrs. Roosevelt. "It may have had nothing to do with her personally."

"For what *reason?*" the professor demanded. "If she wasn't raped and wasn't robbed . . ."

"When we know the answer to that, we'll know who did it," said Mrs. Roosevelt.

"Two young men who had dated her stopped by to pay their respects," said Professor Robinson. "We thought that was kind of them, and if they are the kind of young men she was dating, we feel some assurance about the life she led in Washington. You see, we were reluctant to have her come here. Lucinda had about her a sort of—How shall I say?—*independent* streak. Some of the young men she saw back home were not the kind of young men we wanted her to see. But the ones we met this evening were very nice young fellows."

"Who were they?" asked Mrs. Roosevelt.

"Well, there was a young man here named Bob Grant. An automobile salesman, and a very sympathetic young man. He was polite, and he brought those yellow roses there. He said he'd dated Lucinda for a short while and was horrified to hear about her death."

"And who was the other young man?" asked the First Lady. "What was *his* name?"

"He was very nice, too," said the professor. "I suppose we wouldn't have wanted him for a son-in-law. Jewish fellow, I gathered. Though maybe not. I didn't ask him, and he didn't say. He stood in front of her over there and cried. Great big tears ran down his cheeks. It seemed like he was just genuinely grieving over Lucinda."

"What was his *name*, Professor?"

"His name was Lasky," said Professor Robinson. "David Lasky. It's there in the book. He signed the book."

But he hadn't. David Lasky had not signed the book.

IV

Ed Kennelly caught up with Professor and Mrs. Robinson after they had already taken their seats in a coach of the train back to Minnesota. He had shown his badge to the conductor and asked him to hold the train a few minutes.

"Professor Robinson, Mrs. Robinson," he said. "I'm sorry to have to disturb you at such a time. I simply need to show you a photograph." He handed the couple a small snapshot. "Do you know who that is?"

Both frowned, and the professor nodded. "That's David Lasky. That's the young man who came to the funeral home last evening and cried over Lucinda."

"Thank you," said Kennelly. "My sympathy once again. I'll let you know as soon as we solve the mystery."

"Don't you think, Captain, that we are entitled to an explanation of why you showed us this picture?"

Kennelly hesitated for a moment, then said, "We were afraid David Lasky might have been killed, too."

In the First Lady's office an hour later, Kennelly sat down with Mrs. Roosevelt and Jerry Baines.

"It was David Lasky, all right," he said. "The professor picked up on the snapshot right away. So the guy's not dead. And he hasn't lammed far."

"It took some nerve, I'd think, to show up at that funeral home last night," said Baines.

"It took something else," said Mrs. Roosevelt. "Access to information. I don't believe the newspapers have reported even yet that Lucinda's body had been removed from the morgue and taken to a funeral home, much less to *what* funeral home. I have to wonder how he knew."

"I wonder how he knew there would be no police presence at the funeral home," said Baines.

"There was," said Kennelly. "He walked in and walked out. Right past my man. Walked right into the room and shook hands with the professor. Stood at the casket for a while. Then came out and hovered over the book as if he was signing. Walked out. My guy wasn't looking for Lasky, never figured he'd have the guts to—Anyway, he seemed to know the Robinsons, and he was all tearful. But you're right. It took guts, and it took smarts."

"Or maybe he really loved the girl," said Mrs. Roosevelt. "Isn't that possible?"

"I have more information for you," said Kennelly. "The fingerprints on the second flower card. The one we found at her house. Yours and hers, Ma'am. Whoever wrote those two cards did not leave his prints on 'em."

"I've been thinking about that," said the First Lady. "Shouldn't there have been the fingerprints of someone in the florist shop?"

"Should have been," said Kennelly.

"What's more," she said, "the cards had no names printed on them. Don't the cards from flower shops usually have the name of the florist printed on them? I can think of only one explanation: that he brought his own cards and asked the florist to put *them* with the flowers."

"Which would mean he was trying to hide his identity," said Kennelly. "Which means he was planning to kill her."

"I'm not sure I'd go quite so far as that," said Mrs. Roosevelt. "But it's not unreasonable to think so."

Edith Benham Helm was well qualified to be the social secretary to the First Lady. She had performed the same service for Mrs. Woodrow Wilson, and Mrs. Roosevelt had felt herself fortunate in being able to persuade her to return to the White House in 1933. Later that morning, after Baines and Kennelly had left, Mrs. Helm came to the second floor.

"I believe I have been amiss, Eleanor," she said. Very few people in official positions called Mrs. Roosevelt by her first name, but Mrs. Helm knew she was welcome to. "Two of the most significant events of my life happened last week, and I was so much focused on the one that I gave too little attention to the other."

"I'm not sure I follow," said Mrs. Roosevelt.

"The royal visit and the death of poor Lucinda. I guess I actually failed to get it straight in my head that the poor, dear child was dead—until I went to the funeral parlor last night and saw her. That made me realize I hadn't really thought through the questions that were asked me."

"I can well understand," said Mrs. Roosevelt sympathetically. "You've been carrying heavy responsibilities."

"The royal visit . . . Well, I had never believed I would have a role in entertaining *their majesties.*" She paused and smiled. "Any majesties. I suppose my fascination with it should have abated after they left Hyde Park station. But— I've spent much time this week writing a detailed account of how the visit was handled, what went right, what went wrong, for the benefit of the next social secretary—and, for that matter, the next chief usher and so on—who has to receive royalty. Also, there were notes to send. Thank-you notes. A few notes suggesting to suppliers of goods and services how their part could have been done better. Anyway . . . Last night, staring at the body of that unfortunate young woman, it occurred to me that I hadn't given enough attention to last Thursday morning, perhaps not also to things that happened before."

"Have you thought of something that might be helpful, Edith?"

"I don't know. But I thought I should bring you my best judgment as to when Lucinda disappeared."

"I should appreciate having that," said Mrs. Roosevelt.

"Also, exploring my memory, thinking very closely about it, I did recall seeing her in conversation with one or two other young men—besides David Lasky, I mean."

"I must confess, I do wish you had told me sooner," said Mrs. Roosevelt. "On the other hand . . . perhaps no harm."

Edith Helm frowned and nodded. "Thursday morning," she said, "Lucinda came up to report to you. That would have been a little after nine, if I recall correctly."

"Between nine and nine-thirty," Mrs. Roosevelt agreed.

"I remember her returning. She was at her desk at, say, a quarter till ten. And after that. I've been trying to relate events of the morning to when I last saw her. I am going to say I never saw her again after ten-fifteen."

"Was it unusual for Lucinda to be away from her desk for very long?"

"Not last week," said Mrs. Helm. "It was such a hectic time! Ordinarily I would have been more conscious of where she was and what she was doing. But I trusted her, you understand. I was never concerned that Lucinda Robinson was off somewhere loafing. She was a conscientious worker."

"She hoped to enter the diplomatic service, eventually," said Mrs. Roosevelt.

"Oh, I know. She spoke fluent German. I'm no judge of that, but it is my understanding that she spoke absolutely perfect German. I knew she wouldn't stay on as my assistant for very long. She was ambitious. She meant to climb high. Or to marry well."

"I've heard nothing about any ambitions with respect to marriage," said the First Lady.

"Oh, she had very firm ideas about marriage," said Mrs. Helm. "She told me she was a little girl from not-very-good antecedents in Minnesota but that she meant to marry—if ever she married—into wealth and position. She smiled when she said it, but it was obvious she meant it. Professor and Mrs. Robinson impressed me as fine people; and I had to remember, as I thought about it last night, how Lucinda spoke of a humble background that she was going to escape."

"It is my understanding," said Mrs. Roosevelt, "that David Lasky is the heir to some money. I hardly think, though, that he would represent wealth and position. A young lawyer from Florida. Well . . . Maybe. Have you any idea about other young men?"

"She spent more time on the telephone than her job perhaps really required—though never so much that I felt I should say anything to her about it. I suspect, now that I think of it, that she was talking to men."

"But you can't identify any of them?"

"I saw her in the arcade between the East Wing and the White House once, talking earnestly to a very handsome young man. I have no idea who he was or that he and she were talking about anything but something related to her job."

"We're looking for someone who spoke German and sent her flowers," said Mrs. Roosevelt. "He wrote the accompanying notes in German. I should very much like to know who he is."

Mrs. Helm nodded thoughtfully. "A German . . . I've no idea

who he might be. Maybe he is not a German. Maybe he's someone in the diplomatic service, on whom she was practicing her German. On the other hand— I don't think she needed to practice it. She was fluent."

"But maybe not idiomatic," said Mrs. Roosevelt. "Perhaps she was learning current German idiom, which I am sure is somewhat different from what you learn in a German-speaking American home and then in college."

"Well . . . Oh, there is one more thing I can tell you about Lucinda. She was short of money."

"Indeed?"

"Yes. Twice I overheard telephone conversations when she was obviously telling someone she would settle her account presently. She was oddly impatient with whomever was on the other end of the line during those calls. She was anything but deferential, anything but pleading."

"Government service does not pay very well," said Mrs. Roosevelt.

"If you think about it," said Mrs. Helm, "she dressed quite well, more expensively than you might expect of a young woman in her position."

"More expensively than you know," said the First Lady. "Her evening wear was quite beautiful, and not cheap."

"Well, you have a question there," said Mrs. Helm. "Where did she get the money?"

"You must be there, Babs," the President had said about the luncheon and ceremony for that Wednesday. A luncheon would be followed by a press conference on the lawn.

She understood. Her reputation was for being deeply concerned about things the American people should be deeply concerned about—and perhaps insufficiently interested in things they really did care about. The luncheon, in the private dining room, was to honor Lou Gehrig, who was retiring from baseball after an outstanding fourteen-year career, because he had been stricken with a strange and crippling disease.

Mrs. Roosevelt was aware of the name Gehrig, and also of the name Ruth, the man who would accompany Gehrig to the luncheon; but she took the trouble to review the careers of both men before she sat down over lunch with them. Gehrig, she learned, had been a fine all-'round player but had set a record that might never be broken—he had played in 2,130 consecutive games between 1925 and 1939. Ruth was designated, simply, as the greatest baseball player of all time.

Mrs. Nesbitt telephoned late in the morning. "The President doesn't like our menu," she said somewhat petulantly.

"What is our menu?" the First Lady asked.

"Tuna salad, celery and carrot sticks, sliced cucumbers and tomatoes, and iced tea."

"And what does the President want?"

"Steaks and beer," said Mrs. Nesbitt.

"Steaks and beer it must be," said Mrs. Roosevelt. "Be careful that the steaks not be overdone."

The two baseball players were accompanied by Yankee manager Joe McCarthy. Gehrig and McCarthy wore summerweight suits with white shirts and neckties. The broad-faced, broad-beamed Ruth wore a beige double-breasted suit with no necktie, his collar tips lying on the lapels of his suit.

This was the kind of occasion the President enjoyed, and he drew his wheelchair up to the table and lifted a glass of beer in toast. "To the Iron Man and the Babe," he said. "Two fellows who make us remember what this country is really all about."

Babe Ruth grinned and downed half his glass in response to the toast. Lou Gehrig was somewhat less exuberant, though no outward sign of his disease was yet showing.

"Well, gentlemen, I have seen both of you play. Not as many times as I could have wished."

"We remember ya throwin' out the first ball a couple times, Prez," said Ruth. "When you was governor."

"One of the home runs I saw you hit, I thought was just for me," said the President. "It went over my head like a cannon ball. If it had been twenty feet lower, it'd have taken my head off."

"Oh, I wouldn't do that," said Ruth innocently.

"I'm sorry you have to retire, Lou," said the President. "Life deals us some pretty sorry hands sometimes."

"I wouldn't ask for any hand but the one that was dealt me, Mr. President," said Gehrig. "I'm a very lucky man."

"We all are, I figure," said Babe Ruth. "Look at us around this table. Every one of us has been able to do for a living the thing we most love to do in this life. You couldn't ask God for more than that, could ya?"

"That's a marvelous philosophy, Mr. Ruth," said the First Lady.

"Well, I don't know for sure what a philosophy is, Mrs. Prez," said Ruth. "All I know is, I got dealt a pretty good hand, and Lou and Joe did, and I bet you and Mr. Roosevelt figure you wuz too."

"I think I better issue a commendation," said Kennelly. "My guys have done pretty quick work."

"Quick, indeed," said Mrs. Roosevelt. "So what have we learned?"

"Well . . . After you called this morning, I sent one of my young guys, Fred Mariott, to look into Lucinda Robinson's bank account. The bank cooperated and didn't require a court order. They even photocopied these statements for us."

The First Lady scanned the bank statements. On the first and fifteenth of each month, Lucinda had deposited $59.27, her biweekly paychecks. From time to time, over the past several months, however, she had also deposited odd amounts at odd times. Two weeks ago, $50.00; five weeks ago, $100; six weeks ago, $20.00. She had written regular checks for her room and board, occasional checks for cash, and frequent checks to stores.

"Fred went to two of those shops," said Kennelly. "She'd run up an account of over two hundred dollars at Amberg's. The balance last week was $85.75. They acknowledged that she was a good customer but said they worried about payment. She'd miss two or three payments, then give them fifty dollars or so all at once. She bought nothing cheap."

"You can't buy anything cheap at Amberg's," said Mrs. Roosevelt.

"If you study the checks, you can match them to the irregular deposits," said Kennelly. "It looks like whenever she was being dunned by stores, she somehow got in some extra money and wrote checks against her accounts."

"It could have been the other way, of course," said Mrs. Roosevelt. "Maybe she made the payments whenever she got extra money. Maybe she got checks from home. Maybe she owned a little property somewhere."

"The irregular deposits were always in cash," said Kennelly.

"What is the total?" she asked.

"For the year she was in Washington, $330."

"Not a very great amount of money," Mrs. Roosevelt suggested. "It would be difficult to think she was engaged in some sort of criminal activity."

"That is what she deposited and wrote checks on," said Kennelly. "How do we know she didn't get twice that much more, in cash?"

The First Lady shook her head. "I'm afraid we *don't* know, Captain Kennelly," she said. "I am afraid we don't know."

* * *

The President was in an ebullient mood. He had decided to be, was determined to be. During the day he had received ominous news. A representative of the British Foreign Office, William Strang, had arrived in Moscow to meet with Soviet Foreign Minister Vyacheslav Molotov, to work for the establishment of a peace front in Eastern Europe: an entente among the Soviet Union, France, and Britain. Strang was a low-ranking diplomat. Foreign Secretary Lord Halifax had refused to go, on the ground that he, a devout Christian and High Churchman, could not negotiate with the godless Communists. Arriving at the Kremlin, Strang had been cordially received by Molotov; but he observed something mysterious in the Foreign Minister's comportment—why, Strang could not imagine. Winston Churchill, who had confidentially communicated all this information to the President, guessed why. Earlier in the day, the Soviet Foreign Minister had been long closeted with Count Friederich Werner von der Schulenberg. Von der Schulenberg was a high-ranking diplomat, so high ranking that dispatch of Strang may have seemed to Molotov like a slap in the face from London. He could smile mysteriously at the British representative. He could even laugh at him behind his back.

What was going on? Hitler, Churchill warned the President, was opening negotiations that might lead to a Nazi-Soviet non-aggression pact. Such a treaty would constitute an immediate threat to the peace of Europe. Winston Churchill was alarmed, and heretofore Churchill had proved consistently right. With the Soviet Union neutralized, Hitler might very well feel confident enough to launch a major war—before the summer was over.

Such gloomy thoughts had occupied the President's mind in the afternoon. He could do nothing about them now and had decided to enjoy a relaxed evening.

Arthur Prettyman, the President's valet, had wheeled in

the table with the bottles, the glasses, the ice, and the shaker. The steel and wood wheelchair was before the couch under the west window of the West Sitting Hall. Missy sat on the couch. So did Harry Hopkins. Pa Watson sat in a chair to one side.

Varying his routine, the President did not mix martinis this evening. Instead, he mixed another favorite cocktail of his: Scotch old-fashioneds. He took joy in the ritual of mulling his sugar, and arranging the fruit in the glasses. As always, he was as precise as a chemist in his measurements, pouring exactly the right amount of whisky, water, and bitters.

Mrs. Roosevelt would be leaving the White House shortly. She was dining that evening with some personal friends, including Lorena Hickock and Joseph Lash. The first drinks had been poured, and Pa Watson had begun to tell a joke when the First Lady emerged from her rooms.

"You are welcome to join us," the President said, knowing full well that she wouldn't. She almost never did. "I have some sherry here."

Mrs. Roosevelt smiled and said, "I will have a small sherry. I have a brief word for Harry."

"I am anxious to hear it," said Harry Hopkins.

"Well . . ." She waited until the President had poured her half a glass of dry sherry and handed it to her. She sat down with it. "You know your young lawyer, David Lasky—"

"Is missing," Hopkins interrupted. "Is suspected of having murdered Lucinda Robinson. Or may be dead himself."

"He is not dead himself, Harry," she said. "That is what I wanted to tell you. He appeared last night at the funeral home and wept over Lucinda."

"My god! Was he arrested?"

"No. A police officer was there but did not recognize him."

Hopkins sighed. "I'm glad to hear he's not dead. Frankly, Eleanor, I can't believe Dave Lasky could possibly have

killed Lucinda Robinson. I understand the body was moved
to the third floor. Did you ever see Dave? He's a *little* fellow.
Slight. I don't think he could have lifted her."

"I see you are playing Hawkshaw the Detective again,
Babs," said the President. He said it jovially and yet with an
underlying sharpness that reminded her he was always
afraid she would embarrass him by meddling in police investigations.

"An important part of my role is to keep the matter subdued," she said.

The President chuckled. "If the press ever gets wind of the
extent to which you involve yourself in these things, the out-
break of war in Europe will be driven off the front pages."

"Dave Lasky is a fine young lawyer, Eleanor," said Hopkins.

"I have no doubt of it. I understand he is heir to some
money."

"Not exactly," said Hopkins. "His father is alive and sends
him money. Ask me what business his father is in."

"What business is his father in?"

Hopkins smiled. "He operates a carpet joint in Fort Lau-
derdale."

"Do you mean he sells—?"

"No. A carpet joint is a roadhouse, with gambling. It's up-
scale from a saloon and is called a carpet joint because the
floors are covered with carpet instead of sawdust."

"Are you telling us, Harry, you hired the son of a gangster
to work in the White House?" the President asked.

"No. Gambling is against the law, but Sam Lasky operates
an honest house, with no cheating, no prostitution on the
premises, and no rough stuff. I had the FBI check him out
before I hired Dave. Even if Sam had been a crook, I might
still have hired Dave. He didn't go into the business. He didn't
want to, but his father wouldn't have let him if he had."

"You've seen this place? Do you know this man?" asked the First Lady.

Hopkins nodded. "I had occasion to be in Florida. I drove up and had a look at the place. Sam Lasky recognized me and treated me to dinner. He thanked me for being so kind to his son."

"I see a problem," said the President.

"So do I," said Hopkins. "If Dave Lasky is identified as a suspect in the murder of Lucinda Robinson, the baying hounds of the Republican newspapers will set up a howl that will be heard on the moon."

"He has not been identified so far," said Mrs. Roosevelt. "The word given to the press has been that there is no suspect."

"Where is he?" asked Hopkins. "Do you have any idea?"

Mrs. Roosevelt shook her head. "He can't be far away, since he appeared at the funeral home last evening."

"Do you want me to find him for you?"

"How would you do that, Harry?"

"I'll telephone his father. I'm not a gambling man, but I'll bet anything his father knows where the boy is."

"I should appreciate your doing so, Harry," said Mrs. Roosevelt. "In the meantime, I shall advise Captain Kennelly of the importance of keeping the young man's name confidential."

"Which will be possible," said the President, "only if in fact he didn't kill Lucinda Robinson. You have to find evidence to prove he didn't, Hawkshaw."

"I have never thought he did. But of course, if we find evidence that he did, we can't suppress it."

"Correct. You can't. But let's hope you don't find that kind of evidence."

"The whole matter will be neatly resolved," said Missy, "when you find out who actually did do it."

* * *

After the First Lady was gone, the President grinned at Harry Hopkins and said, "Went to see this joint, did you? I never cease to be amazed at the breadth of your knowledge and experience."

"Is a carpet joint really any better than a speakeasy?" Missy asked.

"Depends on the speakeasy," said Hopkins. "Look. People want to drink, so during Prohibition there were speakeasies. They were illegal, technically, but millions of Americans patronized them. People want to gamble. It's illegal, but millions of people patronize carpet joints."

"Tell us about the place," said the President.

"The night I was there," said Hopkins, "Jimmy Durante was the entertainer. Coming in the next week was Joe E. Lewis. You know the story about Lewis? In Chicago, in 1927, some gangsters beat him nearly to death. He knew who did it, but he wouldn't say. The police could never get it out of him. As a direct result, Joe E. Lewis has never been without work a day since. He's not the world's greatest comedian, but the guys take care of him."

"I thought you said Lasky is not a gangster," said Missy.

"I don't think he is. But there have to be contacts. What's a gangster anyway? Was everyone who sold illegal liquor a gangster? Is everyone who offers illegal gambling a gangster? Sam Lasky was a gentleman when I met him. And his son certainly is."

"Someone's hiding him," said Missy.

"I guess so."

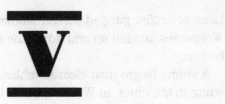

V

"Uh . . . 'Detective Broderick,' would you like to assist me in interviewing a possible witness?" Ed Kennelly asked the First Lady early on Thursday morning.

On the way to the Exeter Diner, where they would meet with this witness, Kennelly explained that Detective Fred Mariott, the man who had obtained copies of Lucinda Robinson's bank accounts, had identified a man who had paid Lucinda's account at a lingerie shop called La Femme. He had paid by check, and the detective had contacted him last evening. Anxious not to be arrested, even to be seen at police headquarters, the witness had agreed to meet Captain Kennelly at the Exeter Diner at 9:30.

The diner was meant to represent the retired trolley car that had often become a diner in the past two or three decades. In fact, it had been built on the lot, and only the counter and booths were in the long, carlike front, while a kitchen and walk-in refrigerator were in an ordinary square building attached behind. Two men and a woman in grease-spattered white clothes labored behind the counter at hot grills, turning sausages and bacon and eggs with big spatulas.

Urns of coffee gurgled. Bread smoked in six-slot toasters. Waitresses hurried up and down the counter and out to the booths.

A young Negro man cleared tables. He was the only non-white in the diner. In Washington in 1939, white people and people of color did not eat in the same restaurants.

As soon as they were inside, Kennelly stood at the door and looked around. He spotted Detective Fred Mariott sitting in a booth to the right and walked toward that booth, followed by Mrs. Roosevelt.

"H'lo, Fred. This your man?"

"Right, Captain. Martin Willoughby."

Martin Willoughby looked up and smiled tentatively, nervously. He was, as Kennelly guessed, about forty years old. He was English in appearance: apple-cheeked, sandy-haired, meticulously dressed in a vaguely out-of-style suit, muscular and yet a little pudgy.

"So, Mr. Willoughby ... Let me introduce Detective Martha Broderick."

A curious half-smiling frown came over Willoughby's face as he nodded at Mrs. Roosevelt. He could not stand up to greet her, since he was on the window side of the booth, with Mariott between him and the aisle.

"Well . . ." said Kennelly. "We understand you wrote a check. Let's see, a check dated May 3. To pay an account that belonged to Lucinda Robinson. Do you want to tell us why?"

Willoughby shrugged. "It's nothing very complicated," he said.

"Okay. So, why?"

"She was— For a while, she was my girlfriend."

"It might be well," said Mrs. Roosevelt, lowering her voice a register to create the persona of Detective Broderick, "if we began at the beginning. Please tell us, Mr. Willoughby, who you are. What do you do for a living?"

"I sell insurance," said Willoughby. "I guess I'm not much of anybody in particular. I live alone, and I sell insurance. I met Lucy at a party. She seemed a lonely girl. I'm a lonely man. So I invited her to go out with me."

"And she did," said Kennelly.

"She did."

"And . . . ?"

"We hit it off. I thought we did. She was very bright, you know. Exceptionally intelligent. I— Well . . . The usual thing happened. I seriously thought of asking her to marry me."

"You seriously thought of it, but you didn't?"

"No. I had to be aware that I wasn't the only man she was seeing. I mean . . . This was odd, you know? Here she was, the apparently innocent little girl from Minnesota, come to Washington to work and learn, and she was seeing lots of men, not just one or two, as I figured out."

"And asking them for money," said Kennelly.

"She asked me if I could help her out with that bill," said Willoughby. "I stopped in the shop one day, asked how much it was, and gave them a check for $54.85. She told me she'd pay it back, but she never offered to."

"Maybe she never got around to it," suggested Detective Broderick.

"That's possible. Possible . . . But for the past month or two she was preoccupied. I think she had started seeing somebody that had gotten to be special to her. She made it clear she really didn't have time for me."

"Who do you think this somebody special might be?" asked Kennelly.

They paused while a waitress took their orders. They ordered coffee, and Ed Kennelly ordered a cheese Danish.

"I wish I knew," said Willoughby.

"Did she ever speak of a German friend?" asked Detective Broderick.

Willoughby shook his head. "The only man she ever spoke about was this fellow Lasky . . . and he's not what he seems to be."

"What do you mean by that?" asked Kennelly.

"He's supposed to be a bright young lawyer from Florida. The truth is, he's from New York, and his father is the operator of a string of gambling casinos and bawdy houses. One of *those* is in Florida."

"How do you know that?" asked Detective Broderick.

Willoughby lifted his chin. "Well . . . in the insurance business you have ways of finding out things."

"Who do you think killed her?" asked Kennelly.

"All I know about that is what I read in the newspapers," said Willoughby.

"May I ask a question, sir?" Detective Mariott asked Kennelly. The young detective was a handsome, brown-haired man, intent and deferential.

"Sure."

"You say, Mr. Willoughby, that Miss Robinson asked you to help her with a clothing bill—"

"Lingerie bill. Lacy flimsies."

"A lingerie bill. Did she tell you why she couldn't pay her bill?"

"Uh, well— I'd said something about how pretty the things she wore were, and she told me she'd gone overboard buying things she thought I'd like and was having difficulty paying the bill."

"So you saw these garments," said Mariott soberly.

"Yes. Yes, I did. Our relationship was the kind where— She visited my apartment."

"Did you think you'd seen $54.85 worth of intimate underthings?"

"How do I know what stuff like that costs?"

"Did she ask you to go in the shop and pay her bill, or did she ask you to give her the money to pay the bill?"

"In point of fact, she asked for the money."

"The exact amount?"

Willoughby drew a breath. "She asked for a hundred dollars."

Mariott nodded. "Did you get any sense that Miss Robinson was a . . . That she was a tramp?"

Willoughby shook his head firmly. "I wouldn't say that."

"But you knew she was asking other men for money."

"I knew Lasky gave her money."

"For what? Why?"

Willoughby scowled. "To sleep with him," he muttered. "Why else would she? The little weasel!"

"Which makes her what?" asked Mariott.

"You want me to say it? It makes her a hooker!"

"Is that what she was?" asked Detective Broderick.

Willoughby lowered his chin and for a moment closed his eyes. "I don't know," he said miserably.

After Martin Willoughby left the diner, Kennelly called for the manager. He showed his badge.

"Kennelly. D.C. police. Homicide. I'd like a little box. I'm gonna take a water glass and a cup and a spoon to headquarters for a fingerprint check. Somebody'll bring 'em back. That is, somebody'll bring 'em back if we don't have to hold 'em for evidence."

The President would have liked to leave the White House at noon, to take lunch with friends, a member of Congress, anybody. His schedule made that difficult, and the elaborate efforts required to move him made it triply difficult. Consequently he ate most of his lunches at his desk, from a tray—usually a simple sandwich with an apple or a peach, with coffee or iced tea.

Mrs. Roosevelt rarely joined him at lunch. She knew he didn't want her. She simply could not resist her drive to bring to his attention a thousand urgent things. When she did join him, she did what she did when she came in during her breakfast: came with a notepad with a scribbled list. He listened to her appeal as he finished his breakfast, gladly, but over his spartan tray at lunch he wanted a quarter of an hour's respite. Often, only Fala was with him at lunch, and the effervescent Scottie would scamper around the Oval Office, grateful for his master's attention and more grateful yet for the scraps of sandwich his master always gave him. The President talked to Fala as if the dog were a little person. Fala never interrupted him and of course never contradicted. The President told Fala what he was worried about. Fala listened. Sometimes the dog turned his head sideways and seemed to concentrate. The President was convinced Fala understood more than anyone but himself gave him credit for.

"I am reluctant to interrupt your lunch, Franklin, but there is something I think you should know. Can I bring in Captain Kennelly?"

"Got to do with the murder has it? Okay. Let's hear it."

Ed Kennelly entered the Oval Office reluctantly, with a sense that he was intruding. It was not the first time he had been there, not the first time he had met the President; but he always had a sense that he was coming in where he shouldn't be, taking time he shouldn't take.

"Come in, Ed! Good to see you again. Sit down."

Mrs. Roosevelt had already taken a chair facing the desk, and Kennelly took another.

"I think you should tell the President what we have learned," the First Lady said to Kennelly.

"Well, sir," said Kennelly. When he spoke to the President he was always more conscious than usual of his Irish accent. "As you know, we've been lookin' into the murder of Miss Lucinda Robinson."

"Yes, and I'm sure my wife has explained why it is important that we keep the Lasky name out of it unless he is the guilty party."

"I understand, sir. We are conductin' ourselves accordin'. But something has come up that the lady here thinks deserves your personal attention."

"Go on then, Ed."

"Well, sir. It would seem that Miss Lucinda Robinson was not the innocent lass she appeared. We have heard her described as everything from a saint to a prostitute. I feel certain she was not the latter. But she does seem to have kept company with more than one or two young men in the past year, and from two of them, at least, she received money."

"Money? Indeed!"

The President passed a scrap of sandwich to Fala, who took it, gulped it down, and set off on a run around the office.

"One of the men who gave her money did it by payin' a bill of hers at a certain lingerie shop. He paid by check, which led us to discover his name. We met with him this morning to ask a few questions. A somewhat unusual man, he turned out to be. We met in a diner. When he left, we gathered up everything he had touched and carried them in for fingerprint examination. He said his name is Martin Willoughby. And that is his name all right. He told us he is an insurance salesman. And that is not true. Mr. Martin Willoughby is an agent of the Federal Bureau of Investigation."

"One of John Edgar Hoover's boys?" asked the President.

"I think . . . I think he's one of Mr. Hoover's *agents*, not one of his boys, Mr. President. If you make the distinction."

The President grinned. "I do make it."

"There is something more, Franklin," said Mrs. Roosevelt. "When the D.C. police sent the fingerprints to the FBI to be matched, the Bureau responded they had no such fingerprints on record. Fortunately, the police department had an independent record of those fingerprints."

"I imagine we can only speculate as to what that means," said the President.

"The Bureau lied, Mr. President," said Kennelly grimly.

"What? Saint Edgar's boys *lied?* Fancy that!"

"What is the significance of it?" asked Mrs. Roosevelt.

"I can think of two possibilities," said the President. "Maybe Mr. Willoughby was indiscreet and prevailed on somebody at the Bureau to lie for him, to cover that indiscretion from the Director as well as everybody else. Or maybe the FBI had some sort of interest in Miss Robinson and sicced an agent on her. That's just two possibilities. I imagine we can think of more."

"I will say this," said Kennelly. "If J. Edgar Hoover found out that one of his agents was paying for scanty undies for a girl he wasn't married to, that agent would be in trouble."

"He's very puritanical about everybody's conduct but his own," said the President.

"I can think of another possibility," said Mrs. Roosevelt. "Is it not possible that Director Hoover would like to have inside informants in the White House? Is it not possible that Mr. Willoughby was assigned to worm his way into a close relationship with Lucinda in the hope she would prove a source of information about doings in the White House?"

"An assistant to the First Lady's *social secretary?*" the President asked with a skeptical grin.

"Director Hoover," said Mrs. Roosevelt, "would like to discover that I am secretly a Communist. Or something."

The President paused for a moment. "Well . . ."

"I can think of only one way to resolve the problem," she said. "A confrontation between Mr. Willoughby and *you*. No one else would carry sufficient weight to force him to answer honestly."

"No one else could make him snitch on Edgar, you mean."

"Put it that way," said Mrs. Roosevelt.

"Can you set it up?"

Kennelly nodded. "I'll tell Willoughby, the 'insurance salesman,' that we need to talk to him again. Then I'll bring him here. Whenever you want him."

"Five o'clock," said the President.

Since Ed Kennelly had spent most of his lunch hour with the President, Mrs. Roosevelt asked him to have lunch with her in the White House. If he expected something grand, he was soon wholly disillusioned, because she took him down to the kitchen and asked the staff to set up a lunch of sandwiches on the big table used for food preparation. They lunched on ham and cheese sandwiches, with iced tea. They were joined by Jerry Baines.

"It occurs to me that the murder is now a week old and we still don't know where it happened," said the First Lady.

"Not for want of trying to find out," said Baines. "Obviously there were no eyewitnesses."

"Maybe there were," she said. "We've assumed that one person killed Lucinda and one person carried the body upstairs. The case would take on a different complexion, wouldn't it, if two or even three people took part in it?"

"Until we can figure out a motive, we can only guess about that," said Kennelly.

Mrs. Roosevelt began to doodle on a piece of paper. She wrote—

WHEN
After 10:15

WHERE
?

WHY
???

Having finished their sandwiches, the First Lady and the two men walked east through the center hall of the ground floor.

Like the West Wing, which houses the Oval Office, the East Wing is a separate building, connected to the White House by an arcade. They continued east through the arcade. Short of the entrance to the East Wing they stopped and talked.

The arcade was a beautiful place. It had long been the First Lady's thought that the land to the south should be made a garden like the rose garden that bordered the colonnade between the White House and the West Wing. The East Wing was a bit more distantly separated from the White House than was the West Wing, and there was plenty of room where flowers could be planted. As it was, the arcade overlooked lawn and trees, and a fresh summer breeze blew through.

"Not many people know this," said Mrs. Roosevelt, "but in 1934 the East Wing was rebuilt, and a bomb shelter was constructed beneath it. That is connected by a tunnel to the Treasury Building on East Executive Avenue."

"The tunnel is a secret escape route from the White House," said Baines. "If the President wants to see someone and doesn't want the press to know about it, the person can come in and go out through the tunnel. Of course, the doors are locked. You can't go through the tunnel unless someone unlocks the doors for you."

"Who has keys to those doors?" asked Mrs. Roosevelt.

"Well . . . *I* have one," said Baines. "Several of the Secret Service agents have one. Some of the White House police. Louis Howe had a key."

"Is the tunnel much used?" asked Kennelly.

"Not much," said Baines.

"Well, is it possible," Kennelly asked, "that Miss Robinson was for some reason lured into the bomb shelter, murdered there, and her body hidden there, while the murderer escaped through the tunnel?"

"That's quite possible, I'd think," said Baines.

"One fact argues against the idea," said Mrs. Roosevelt. "If the body was hidden in the bomb shelter, where it was unlikely it would be found for some time, then why was it taken from there and moved to the linen closet on the third floor?"

"Another question for your set of notes," said Baines.

"Yes, indeed. Another question. Why did someone move the body to a place where it was bound to be discovered when the linen was gathered up to be laundered?"

"A very good question," Kennelly grunted.

"I have to wonder," said Mrs. Roosevelt, "if the answer

doesn't in some way relate to the royal visit. The murderer, for some reason, didn't want the body found—that is to say, did not want the murder to be discovered—while the King and Queen were in the White House."

"If he didn't want that to happen, why did he kill her while the King and Queen were here, or about to arrive here?" Kennelly asked.

"That goes to the question of motive," said the First Lady. "May I guess that the perceived necessity of killing her arose suddenly? Something between Lucinda and her killer . . . Something happened suddenly, and he believed the only solution was to kill her."

"He couldn't have killed her in her office or in any of the public parts of the White House," said Kennelly. "That means he some way got her to leave her office and meet him somewhere."

"Thursday morning . . ." said Baines. "I don't remember a busier morning—except maybe the morning when President Harding's body was returned and placed in the East Room."

They walked back through the arcade and into the ground floor of the White House.

"Some of these rooms are little used," said Mrs. Roosevelt, glancing around at the doors to rooms in the east end of the ground floor. "Temporary offices, some of them. The other end of this floor is busy. Physician's office, housekeeper's office, kitchen, and pantry. But this end . . ."

"A body that's been strangled doesn't leave bloodstains," said Kennelly.

"Men's room, powder room," said Mrs. Roosevelt, pointing to doors on either side of the hall. "Some sort of temporary work is going on in this room." She nodded toward the open door of a large room, where a staff of four or five people were busily shuffling papers. "I'm not sure exactly what they are doing."

When the First Lady stepped into the doorway, work in the room stopped.

"Oh, Mrs. Roosevelt, how nice of you to visit us!" exclaimed a woman who rose from behind a table stacked high with paper. "Do come in."

The First Lady glanced at Kennelly and Baines, then walked into the room. "I must confess I am not certain just what it is you are doing," she said.

"These," said the woman, "are archives from 1917 through 1920, the last years of the Wilson Administration. Wartime papers. We are sorting and cataloguing them. A few, believe it or not, are still regarded as confidential. They are put aside for review. The rest of these archives are being sorted chronologically and indexed by subject, in preparation for their move to the National Archives."

"I see. How long will this project take?"

"About ten months, we think. We've worked on it about seven months and can see about three months more work to do. My name is Cynthia Phillips, Mrs. Roosevelt. The young man over there is Christian Cassell. That is Mary Logan, and that is Betty Fulk."

The young people were all in their early twenties. All stood respectfully and smiled at the First Lady. The girls were attractive. The young man was broad-shouldered, muscular, and handsome. He didn't look like the sort of young man who would be working at indexing archives.

"Under what auspices are you here?"

"The N.Y.A.," said Cynthia Phillips. She referred to the National Youth Administration, which employed young people in jobs like this while they were completing their education.

"Well, it's good to see you," said Mrs. Roosevelt.

"We'd like to thank you for last week," said Cynthia Phillips.

"You are very welcome," said Mrs. Roosevelt. She smiled broadly. "But for what?"

"For giving us the opportunity to see the King and Queen," said the young woman.

"Oh, well—"

"Didn't you know? We served as temporary maids and a temporary usher for the royal visit. Betty and Mary and I put on maids uniforms and worked on the second and third floors and helped with the state dinner. Chris worked as an usher. Oh, it was *wonderful!* We all got to see the King and Queen and all the celebrities. You might not believe this, Ma'am, but we had worked in the White House four months, and none of us had ever seen the President before!"

"So," asked Kennelly, "you just suspended operations in this room?"

"Yes, Sir. Wednesday afternoon we were taught what to do, and Thursday and Friday we worked as maids and an usher."

Kennelly glanced hard at Mrs. Roosevelt. She saw what he did: that the cabinets in which the archives were stored were big enough to hold a body. Besides that, there were two closets.

"I am glad you enjoyed the experience," said Mrs. Roosevelt to the four young people. "I am sure the President will want to thank you for your work, when it is finished."

In the hall outside, she said, "We must not jump to conclusions. But . . . it is possible, isn't it?"

In the Oval Office at five o'clock, the President lifted himself from his chair to his wheelchair and rolled over to the couches that stood perpendicular to the fireplace.

"Well, Brother Willoughby, I imagine you are surprised to find yourself here," he said in a jocund voice.

"I am, in fact, Mr. President," said Martin Willoughby.

He was conspicuously apprehensive and sat stiffly on one of the couches, his hands tightly folded in his lap. His collar, which had not looked too tight this morning, was apparently uncomfortably tight now. His straw hat lay on the couch beside him.

"It has come to my attention," said the President, "that you don't really work for an insurance company. The truth is, you work for *me.*"

"For you, Sir?"

"John Edgar Hoover works for me. If you work for him, you work for me. If you tell one of his secrets to me, that's all right; I'm his boss."

"Sir . . . What makes you think I work for the Director?"

"To start with, no one else calls him 'the Director.' Apart from that, your fingerprints tell it. It won't do, Brother Willoughby. 'Fess up."

Willoughby stiffened even more. "All right. I am an agent of the Federal Bureau of Investigation."

"You want to tell us the story, or do you want us to cross-examine you?"

Willoughby glanced at Mrs. Roosevelt, Ed Kennelly, and Jerry Baines, who sat on the couch opposite him. Abruptly he softened and smiled wryly. "Good afternoon, Mrs. Broderick," he said.

Mrs. Roosevelt smiled. "It is good to see you again, Mr. Willoughby."

His gambit having failed to nonplus the First Lady, Willoughby frowned and said, "I suppose you mean the story of me and Lucinda Robinson."

"That's what I had in mind," said the President.

"She didn't know I am an agent," he said. "She accepted my story that I sell insurance for a living. I . . . became quite enamored of her. As you all know, Lucy was not the world's most beautiful woman, but she had fine qualities. I felt very much betrayed when I found out she was seeing other men—in fact, was more interested in them than she was in me. I was bitter. That's the word for it. I was bitter. But of course I didn't kill her. I can account for myself all day on Thursday."

"We took your fingerprints off the dishes you used this morning," said Kennelly. "Why did the FBI tell us it didn't have a record of them?"

"Standard operating procedure," said Willoughby. "The Bureau always denies it has any record of the fingerprints of agents. Your inquiry triggered an internal investigation, though. Someone will be asking where you found my fingerprints."

"I'll lie," said Kennelly. "Maybe."

"Maybe?"

The President spoke. "It really wouldn't do, would it, for John Edgar Hoover to find out you bought fifty dollars worth of silky underduds for a woman who was not your wife?"

Willoughby nodded. "I'd rather the Director didn't find out about that," he said.

"That would be particularly unfortunate," said Baines, "in view of the fact that you have a wife and two children."

Willoughby started, and his mouth fell open.

"The Secret Service has access to all federal personnel records," said Baines.

"You took a devil of a risk, going out with this not-very-attractive girl," said the President.

"You said you met her at a party," said Mrs. Roosevelt. "Was your wife with you at that party?"

"No."

"Do you often go out to parties without your wife?"

"Well, no I don't."

"And you paid for those undies with a check," said Kennelly. "That's odd conduct for a man trying to keep a secret."

Willoughby glanced at each of the people he confronted. "This isn't quite fair, is it?" he asked plaintively.

"The various circumstances don't fit together, Brother Willoughby," said the President. "Except one way. One way they fit. The contradictions are not contradictions if you pursued Lucinda Robinson because you were *ordered* to do it. And that, of course, is exactly what happened. You wrote a check for the undies because that way you could file for reimbursement on your expense account. 'Fess up, Brother Willoughby. You were ordered to cozy up to a girl working here in the White House, to give John Edgar Hoover a source of information. It worked all right for a while, but she thought she could catch bigger fish, and she dropped you. I bet the Director wasn't very happy with that."

"Mr. President, you put me in an extremely awkward position!"

"Not at all 'Lieutenant' Willoughby. 'Colonel' Hoover has given you one set of orders. 'General' Roosevelt is giving you another, which is to tell the truth. 'Colonel' Hoover may be put in an awkward position, but you are not. So tell us, why were you ordered to cozy up to Lucinda?"

"You're right, Mr. President. The Director wants a source of information within the White House," said Willoughby miserably.

"An assistant to my wife's social secretary . . . He must be desperate."

"The Director believes that Mrs. Roosevelt may have certain social contacts that could be a matter of concern, in the interests of national security."

"John Edgar flatters you, Babs," said the President. "Now, tell me, Brother Willoughby, does John Edgar have other worms in the woodwork around here?"

"I wouldn't know, Mr. President. I wouldn't be told. That's not the way the Director works."

"But you wouldn't be surprised?"

Willoughby sighed. "No, Sir. I wouldn't be surprised."

"I'm going to let you and the Director off the hook," said

the President grimly. "On a condition. From now on, I have a worm in the woodwork at FBI headquarters. You. I want a weekly report, detailed and in writing, of everything you see, hear, or suspect. Now, of course, the fatter that file of reports gets, the deeper you're in trouble with the Director. So be circumspect, Brother Willoughby. Be circumspect. Let's don't let John Edgar find out."

Willoughby's face burned deep red. "I . . . He'll find out, sooner or later."

"That depends on how good you are," said the President.

"Now, Mr. Willoughby," said Mrs. Roosevelt, "we need not take any more of the President's time. We can meet elsewhere, and you can tell us what you know about Lucinda's death."

VI

Among the telegrams for the President's attention that Thursday morning was another from Winston Churchill. Churchill had begun to send the President letters and cables with some regularity in the spring of 1939. The President took them as an embarrassment at first, because this fellow Churchill was not only a renegade politician, not only outside the British cabinet but banished from it, but he made no secret of his desire to influence the President to accept *his* view of European affairs, rather than that of Prime Minister Neville Chamberlain. On reflection, though, the President realized Churchill had been right, most notably about Munich last year; and he began to take Churchill's messages more seriously.

It was particularly interesting to note that Winston Churchill's sources of information were not only far better than the President's own, they were apparently better than those of the Prime Minister. Obviously, Churchill had his own intelligence-gathering network, which supplied him with information the British government obtained only later. Obviously, many men in the Foreign Office and Ministry of

Defence violated their trust and reported to Churchill unpleasant facts they knew would not be welcomed in Whitehall.

It was all very secret and conspiratorial. A few months ago Churchill had sent to the President an apparently innocuous gift: an autographed copy of the Churchill biography of the Duke of Marlborough. Opening the book, the President had discovered that the book had been taken apart, pages replaced, and rebound. The new pages contained a code, which Churchill suggested he would use in cables. Missy had learned the code and deciphered the messages. This morning's message was ominous.

> I am informed from Moscow that, through no fault of his own, Mr. Strang's mission has failed. Messrs. Stalin and Molotov undoubtedly understand that Mr. Chamberlain does not in fact wish to enter into an agreement for the Great Britain to act in concert with France and the Soviet Union to defend Belgium, Greece, Poland etc. against Nazi invasion.
>
> This failure is most ominous for the peace of the world. It undoubtedly means that Stalin has turned to Hitler. If these two murderers elect to work together, they will simply divide up Europe between them. Poland, for example, could not long survive a Soviet-Nazi alliance.

"If he's right," said the President, "a major war could come this summer."

The President shared his bed as usual with Missy and Fala. Missy sat at the foot, eating breakfast from a tray just as the President was doing. Fala sat at the President's side, tail wagging, watching for the bite of toast or bacon that was sure to come.

"Mr. Churchill is called a Cassandra," said Missy.

"Let's fervently hope he is not," said the President. "Do you know who Cassandra was?"

"A doomsayer," Missy said. "A prophet—prophetess, I guess, actually—who always predicted disaster."

"No," said the President. "Cassandra was a prophetess cursed by Apollo. The curse was that her predictions always came true . . . but no one would ever heed them."

Mrs. Roosevelt sat over breakfast with Ed Kennelly and Jerry Baines. Conscious that she was demanding much extra time of them, she tried to compensate in a small way by offering meals. This breakfast was not at the kitchen table downstairs but in the private dining room on the first floor. It was a hearty breakfast, like the one the President always ate— eggs with ham and sausage, toast and marmalade, and coffee.

"Personally," she said, "I remain doubtful that Lucinda was killed by David Lasky. Still, it is a fact that he disappeared, also a fact that he made a brief appearance at the funeral home Tuesday evening. Obviously he is still in Washington, or in the area."

"He's no innocent little lawyer, taken in by a fat little seductress," said Baines. "He knows a lot that we want to know."

"Harry Hopkins said he would telephone Mr. Samuel Lasky," said Mrs. Roosevelt. "I suggest we postpone starting a big search for David Lasky until Harry talks to his father."

That was not a matter long deferred. When Mrs. Roosevelt checked with Harry Hopkins an hour later, Hopkins had already talked to Sam Lasky in Florida.

"He knows the problem," Hopkins said. "He knows his son may be suspected of murder. He's not confident the boy would get a fair trial, because of Sam's reputation. He wasn't willing to tell me where Dave is, but he said he'd call him and urge him to call us. I've given word to the White House switchboard that a call from David Lasky is to be put through to you or me, no matter what."

The call came in before noon. Mrs. Roosevelt was dictating a "My Day" column to Tommy Thompson when the telephone rang and the operator said a Mr. David Lasky was on the line.

"Mrs. Roosevelt?"

"Mr. Lasky?"

"Yes. Is it in fact you, Ma'am? Uh . . . don't bother, please, to have someone try to trace this call. I am calling from a place a long way from where I'm staying."

"I have no intention of doing that, Mr. Lasky. I do want to suggest to you, though, that your sudden disappearance and your continued absence do look bad. They are the only facts, really, that make you a suspect."

"You can imagine how I felt when I realized Lucy was probably dead. I knew she was missing from the White House all Thursday afternoon. I knew she had not been in her room all night. When she did not show up at the White House on Friday morning, I decided something horrible must have happened. I realized that if she had been harmed, I was a very likely suspect. You know who my father is and what he does. For a person like me to be arrested and held in a jail is much more dangerous than it is for some other person."

"Do you suppose you would not have had a fair trial?"

"Worse than that. I might not have survived to come to trial. The name would have meant something to some other prisoners. A cousin of mine was beaten to death in a jail. He was nobody. Just a meat cutter in a butcher shop in Philadelphia."

"Mr. Lasky, tell me how you knew that Lucinda's body had

been removed to a funeral home, and to *what* funeral home."

She could hear a short sigh on the telephone line. Then the young man said, "Mrs. Roosevelt, people like my father . . . so therefore people like me, have friends who watch things and tell us things. It's nothing so unusual. There are men who know where I am and why I am where I am. When it's over, when someone else is convicted of murdering Lucy, I'll come back."

"Are you interested in helping us identify that 'someone else'?"

"Of course. I loved her deeply, Mrs. Roosevelt. I *couldn't* have hurt her."

"Mr. Lasky, who is 'the Kraut'? We found letters of yours referring to someone you called 'the Kraut.' Who is that?"

"I wish I knew. If I'd known, maybe I could have done something about him."

"Why did you call him 'the Kraut'? Is he German?"

"She said he is."

"Did you ever see him?"

"Yes, at a distance. Maybe I should be ashamed to tell this, but I followed Lucy one evening. She met a man in Franklin Park. He was a big, handsome fellow . . . blond. They kissed fervently. Then they walked to Thirteenth Street and caught a cab. When I saw that kiss, I knew . . ."

Mrs. Roosevelt waited for David Lasky to finish his sentence.

". . . she cared more for him, more than she did for me."

"You must forgive my suggestion, Mr. Lasky, that that was a motive for murder."

"Of him, maybe. Not of her."

"Why did you call him an evil man?"

"I suppose because I was so jealous. But she told me things about him. He was a seducer, Mrs. Roosevelt. He was promising her something. I'm not sure what. She said she might not be in Washington much longer, because she had a friend who was going to help her go somewhere she always wanted to be. She was playful about it. I think she enjoyed playing on my jealousy. But she was telling the truth, too. He was promising to take her someplace."

"I believe you gave her money, Mr. Lasky."

"Yes. Lucy was not profligate, but she was not thrifty either. She was not embarrassed to ask for money. She said it was what it cost her to look nice."

"Did she give you reason to think your relationship was permanent, that it might even evolve into marriage?"

"At first she did. Then I realized she had other . . . interests."

"Can I in any way persuade you to come back to the White House?"

"I'd be put in jail. No, there's no way you can persuade me to do that, to take that risk."

"If I could assure you you will not be arrested or charged with murder, will you come back?"

"*Can* you assure me of that?"

"Perhaps not, at the moment. But if I were to arrange for you to speak with the police captain investigating the case, and he assured you, would you come in?"

"I'll have to think about it."

"Telephone me again, Mr. Lasky."

"I will, Ma'am. I'm grateful to you."

Mrs. Roosevelt ate lunch at the Mayflower Hotel, the guest of the Federation of Democratic Women. She was introduced and said a few words, but the main speaker was Frances Perkins, Secretary of Labor.

Miss Perkins was a Bostonian, a graduate of Mount Holyoke, a teacher, a social worker, a longtime lobbyist for reform and consumers' rights, and a member of the New York

Industrial Commission, appointed by Governor Roosevelt. When she was a girl her grandmother had told her emphatically that she should always wear a certain style of tricornered straw hat, since it would overcome the overbroadness of her face. For the rest of her life she never wore any other style of hat—and she wore a hat always.

In her speech, Miss Perkins told a favorite story which Mrs. Roosevelt had heard her tell before. "Two men of charitable proclivity were discussing the question of why a charitable person would give a pair of shoes to a poor man. 'Because his feet are cold,' the first man said emphatically. 'For Jesus' sake,' said the second, just as emphatically. So which was right? I suggest to you that the second was. The worldly humanitarian impulse invariably dies. The recipients of charity seem insufficiently grateful. Resentment arises on both sides. In the best analysis, kindness, compassion, and charity are indeed for Jesus' sake, not for the world's. I remind you of Saint Paul's First Epistle to the Corinthians, in which he said, 'Be ye steadfast, unmovable, always abounding in the work of the Lord, forasmuch as ye know that your work is not in vain in the Lord.' "

While the First Lady was listening to the speech by Secretary of Labor Perkins, Ed Kennelly dropped by the Chevrolet agency where Bob Grant sold cars. Grant was on the floor, and Kennelly leaned against the fender of a '39 Chevy.

"I'm curious about something," said Kennelly. "You told us that Lucinda Robinson had several boyfriends. You didn't say if she had any girlfriends. Surely a young woman living alone in Washington must have had friends, apart from her lovers."

"She lived in the boardinghouse where she lived because a girlfriend of hers lived there and arranged it."

"What was her name?"

"I don't know."

"I asked you before if you knew of any German. Lasky called him 'the Kraut.' "

"She was fascinated with anything German. She used to speak German to me when we were in bed. She'd point to parts of my anatomy and use the German words for them. She'd point at my . . . thing and call it *das männliche Glied.*' That's how she told me about Lasky's. " *'Grösser als das Ihre,*' " she'd say. " *'Ach, so lang, so dick!'* I had to ask her to translate. That last word means 'thick,' incidentally."

"She teased you," said Kennelly.

"Yes, but if you think that means I killed her, forget it."

"But no German boyfriend?"

Grant shook his head. "Not that she ever mentioned to me."

"Which means," said Kennelly to Mrs. Roosevelt in her office that afternoon, "that we have only Lasky's word that there *was* any Kraut. A German. An 'evil man.' Maybe Lasky was setting up a straw man."

"I hardly think," said Mrs. Roosevelt, "he would have set up his straw man by writing Lucinda letters threatening to kill her. Why wouldn't he have just said that *the German* was dangerous and threatened her life? Except for those letters, he wouldn't be a suspect."

"Anyway," said Kennelly, "I went to the boardinghouse and asked the landlord to identify Lucinda's friend. He knew who I meant. He said, sure, she met Lucinda at the White House. Both of them worked there."

"The name?"

"Mary Logan."

"One of the young women working in the Wilson archives," said the First Lady.

"Right."

"I'll send for her."

Mary Logan appeared a few minutes later. She was pretty, with a sharp-featured face and dark hair. She wore a white cotton skirt and a light, short-sleeved, red cotton sweater. The First Lady welcomed her warmly and tried to put her at ease, but the young woman sat stiffly and nervously in the chair she was offered and clasped her hands together so tightly that her knuckles cracked loudly.

"You were a friend of Lucinda Robinson, I believe," said Mrs. Roosevelt.

"Oh, yes. I just can't believe what happened to her."

"Where are you from, Miss Logan, and how does it happen you are working under an N.Y.A. program?"

"I'm from Baltimore, Mrs. Roosevelt. I'm working so I can afford to go to George Washington University. I want to study nursing."

"Do you have any idea who might have killed Lucinda? Or why?"

Mary Logan shook her head. "I've been thinking and thinking. I can't *imagine* why anyone would want to kill her."

"How long had you known her?"

"I met her just after the N.Y.A. sent me here to work. She worked in the East Wing, and occasionally I'd see her walking through into the White House. We spoke and became acquainted. She was interested in what we were doing."

"Where was she living when you met her?"

"In the Bismarck. I told her there was a vacancy in the house where I lived and that she could save money by moving there. So she did."

"Would you say you were *good* friends?"

"We rode to work together on the trolley, every morning. Usually we rode back out together. And we talked. I'd say we got to be very good friends."

"Mary," said Mrs. Roosevelt, "is it true that Lucinda dated frequently—and several young men?"

"Yes. She was very popular."

"Why, do you think?" Ed Kennelly interjected.

Mary Logan hesitated. "She was intelligent . . . out-going . . ."

"Affectionate," suggested the First Lady.

"Yes, I suppose so."

"In fact," said Kennelly, "she was an *accommodating* girl, as you might say. Isn't that true?"

"I understand what you mean," said Mary Logan. "I suppose I have to answer yes."

"She didn't come home every night, did she?" he asked.

Mary Logan sighed. "No, not every night."

"We're not making a judgment of her," said Mrs. Roosevelt. "What she did was her business. It is possible, though, that one of the men she saw became obsessively jealous or found some other reason to want to kill her."

The young woman closed her eyes for a moment. "I've thought of that," she said.

"Did she ever suggest she was worried about something like that?"

Mary Logan shook her head.

"Did you ever meet any of her men friends?"

"Oh, sure. In fact, we double-dated sometimes."

"Bob Grant?" asked Kennelly.

"No. I never met him. Lucinda mentioned him, but I don't think she was still seeing him when I met her."

"David Lasky?"

"Oh, yes. We double-dated with Dave. He had a friend for me, and we went places together."

"Others?"

"Yes. She sometimes went out with a man called Fred Schoenberg. Also, there was a fellow . . . I think she mentioned the name Pitt. Maybe Charles Pitt. Also, uh—"

"Blunt question," Kennelly interrupted. "Did she sleep with those guys, too?"

Mary Logan ran her hands down her face, blowing an audible sigh between her fingers. "If you weren't investigating her death, I wouldn't answer a question like that."

"So what *is* the answer?"

"I don't know for sure, but I wouldn't be surprised."

"In point of fact, Lucinda was promiscuous," said Kennelly. "Wasn't she?"

"In point of fact, Lucinda was a nymphomaniac," said Mary Logan indignantly. "Or almost."

"Oh, did it go that far, really, my dear?" asked Mrs. Roosevelt.

"I suppose I exaggerate," said Mary Logan. "Dave brought Chester Horlick to be my date when we double-dated. The first thing I know, Lucinda is playing up to him, too."

"Did she sleep with him?" asked Kennelly.

"I don't think so," she said but then shrugged and added, "Who knows? She also told me once that she was pregnant. I don't think she really was. I don't know why she said it."

"Who did she say was the father?" asked Kennelly.

"Pitt . . . She said Pitt did it. She said he had money, so it would be all right."

"Very well," said Mrs. Roosevelt crisply. She did not want to carry this line of talk any further. "Did Lucinda tell you that David Lasky wrote her at least two threatening letters?"

Mary Logan shook her head. "My god, no! Threatening . . . ? Dave . . . ?"

"In one letter he specifically threatened to kill her and a man he referred to as 'the Kraut.' Have you any idea who 'the Kraut' might be?"

"Sure. *Sure.* Chris Cassell!"

"You mean Christian Cassell, who works in the archives with you?"

"Yes. I was about to mention him when you asked me if she slept with Fred Schoenberg and Charles—I think it's

Charles—Pitt. She liked Chris a lot. I'm not sure they ever slept together. But she liked him. You see, he can read and speak German, the way she could. In fact, that's why he's working in the Wilson archives. Some of the papers are in German, and his job is to read and catalogue those. She'd step into our room and make little jokes with him in German, which none of the rest of us could understand."

"Were you aware how jealous David Lasky was of him?"

"I had no idea. I knew Dave wanted Lucinda for himself. He asked her to marry him. But . . . To threaten to kill her! And . . . Do you think he *did* it?"

"It's possible," said Mrs. Roosevelt.

"He took it on the lam," said Kennelly. "The day after she was killed, he disappeared."

"But he was at the funeral home! I saw him coming out as I was going in."

"What about Mr. Cassell? Did he go to the funeral home?"

"I don't think so. He may not have known where she was. I knew because the funeral director called the house, saying there were visiting hours and some of us might want to come, so Professor and Mrs. Robinson would not be alone."

"They have no idea what sort of girl she was, do they?" asked Kennelly.

"They have some idea," said Mary Logan. "She didn't suddenly change her ways when she came to Washington, I don't imagine."

"Have you anything else to tell us?" asked Mrs. Roosevelt.

"No, I don't think so."

"Then, thank you, my dear."

"I suppose we've no option but to summon this Mr. Cassell and interrogate him," said the First Lady.

"I see no option," said Kennelly. He indeed saw no option, for if he had he would have absented himself at least long enough to smoke a cigarette. He wanted a cigarette. He needed a cigarette. But he would not smoke in this room. "Are you going to call for him?"

Jerry Baines arrived while they waited for Cassell.

Five minutes later, Christian Cassell came to the First Lady's office and sat down at her invitation. He was deferential but entirely self-confident. Handsome and athletic of build, he confirmed Mrs. Roosevelt's morning judgment that he was not the sort of young man you expected to find cataloging archives.

"It has come to our attention—rather late in the process, I must admit—that you were a close friend of Lucinda Robinson," she said.

Cassell nodded. "She was a charming young woman. I had a great deal of respect for her."

"Blunt question, Mr. Cassell," said Kennelly. "Did you sleep with her?"

Cassell drew a deep breath. "Oh, sir, I . . ." He turned to Mrs. Roosevelt. "Should I answer?" he asked.

"Obviously, the answer is not 'no,' " she said. "You should be as blunt as Captain Kennelly, Mr. Cassell. He is investigating a murder, which is not a gentlemanly business."

Cassell frowned and considered for another moment. Then he nodded. "I should have liked to preserve her reputation, but the answer is yes."

"What reputation is that, you were going to preserve?" Kennelly demanded. "From all we can gather, she didn't have a reputation for virginity."

"I didn't know her reputation. I knew *her*."

"Are you the man David Lasky called 'the Kraut'?"

"I don't know what Lasky called me. I wouldn't be surprised if he called me that. He was insanely jealous of Lucinda. He was possessive, thought he owned her."

"How is it that you speak fluent German, Mr. Cassell?" asked Mrs. Roosevelt.

"I grew up in Columbus, Ohio, in a neighborhood called

German Village. I used to play baseball in Schiller Park. Among the families in the neighborhood were the Rickenbackers. James Thurber's family were neighbors. My grandfather came to this country in 1876. My grandmother came in 1884. They spoke German at home, German only, and speak only a little English even now. My mother speaks broken English. She says things like, 'I'm going to broom the floor.' I talked like that myself until I was sent to school. It was tough at first. The kids laughed at me and called me Dutch. In Ohio, when they say somebody does something 'Dutch,' it means he does it backwards or awkwardly."

"Did you study German in school?" asked Mrs. Roosevelt.

"No, Ma'am. The study of German in the public schools was abolished in 1917 and wasn't restored until I was in high school. Anyway, why would I study German? I already knew it."

"How do you get in and out of the White House?" asked Baines.

"Through the east gate. I come into the East Wing, then walk through the arcade and into the east end of the ground floor."

"Have you ever used the Treasury tunnel?"

Cassell shook his head. "When our group came to work in the White House, we were told to stay in the east end of the ground floor and not go wandering into the other parts of the house. Since we came, security has tightened. Apart from going to the bathroom, I'd never been anywhere in the White House until last week, when I was asked to work for two days as an usher. In fact, I'd thought about taking a tour, to see what the rest of the place is like."

"Who do you think killed her, Mr. Cassell?"

"Ma'am, I have no idea. If I had even a suspicion, I'd tell you immediately. Whoever did it, did a horrible thing."

When Cassell was gone, Kennelly shook his head. "Do you get the feeling like I do that everybody we talk to is lying?"

* * *

That evening the President cut his cocktail hour short and retired to his bedroom early, where Arthur Prettyman helped him to dress in white tie and tails. At seven he left the White House in the presidential limousine and was driven to the Army-Navy Club, where he would address a group of officers, some retired but most active, about the prospects for peace or war.

He had just appointed General George C. Marshall to be Chief of Staff, United States Army, beginning July 1, 1939. At the dinner, which was a stag dinner with all members of the press rigidly excluded, the President sat between General Malin Craig, the outgoing Chief of Staff, and Marshall, the man about to replace him.

"The news from Europe is discouraging," the President said to the two generals. "It looks distinctly possible that Hitler and Stalin are going to sign some kind of alliance."

General Marshall looked at him quizzically.

"I know, George," said the President. "I know what you're going to say. You're going to remind me that our army is smaller than Czechoslovakia's was at the time of Munich."

"Mr. President, we are authorized to have 225,000 men, but we don't even have that many actually in service. *Belgium* has more men under arms than that."

"I know you don't appreciate my emphasizing naval and air strength at the expense of the army, but I am convinced the greatest urgency is in building a powerful navy and air arm. After all, the war will be fought on the other side of an ocean."

"Submarines—" Marshall began.

"Our new fleet submarines will be the finest in the world. Germany did immense damage with submarines in the World War. They—"

"They can't escort ships across the Atlantic," said Marshall.

"What if war comes in the Pacific?" asked the President. "We will blockade Japan, with submarines. In any case, we can expand the army very rapidly by federalizing the National Guard."

"Sir," said Marshall coldly, "General McNair believes the National Guard will be of negligible value in the event of war. It is ill-equipped, ill-trained, and shot through with state politics, which makes its leadership highly dubious."

"You don't say that in public?"

"No, Sir, of course not. But I'm saying it to you."

"Which is a troubling idea," the President said to Missy when Arthur had helped him undress and bathe and to make his way into bed. He had declined a second cognac after dinner with the thought that he and Missy could have one, with coffee, later. He sipped and said, "If he's right, maybe I have miscalculated."

"The Congress would have blocked you on building a bigger army," she said.

"Not this year," he said. "The Congress is ready to rearm the nation—so long as I promise not to send an army overseas."

"What did you say in your speech?" she asked.

"I told them what Churchill has told us—though I didn't use his name, didn't tell them how I'd found out. Marshall said to me later that if the German and Soviet armies were put together, neither France nor Britain nor any other country could withstand them."

"Frightening . . ."

"Of course, that's not what they're going to do," said the President. "They won't fight side by side. Their agreement will just be for each one to stand aside while the other chews off what it wants of the rest of Europe."

"God knows what Hitler wants," said Missy.

"That's an interesting point," said the President. "What he really wants most is western Russia."

"It's going to be an interesting summer," said Missy somberly.

"Remember the old curse," said the President. " 'May you live in interesting times.' "

VII

"Something is obvious," said Mrs. Roosevelt to Gerald Baines on Friday morning. "Whoever killed Lucinda was intimately acquainted with the interior of the White House."

"I certainly agree and have been thinking about it," he said.

"Whoever killed her did it in the White House, hid her body in the White House, and subsequently moved it to the third floor without being seen. That requires knowledge, not only of the physical layout of the house but of its schedule, its comings and goings."

"David Lasky worked in the White House," said Baines.

"I take due note. So, for that matter did Christian Cassell."

They sat together in the First Lady's office, and as Mrs. Roosevelt often did when she asked Baines or Kennelly to meet with her, she had ordered coffee and some assorted pastries. Baines, whose antecedent's, oddly enough for his name, were Belgian, loved coffee and Danish in the earlier half of mid-morning. He munched happily on a cherry Danish, which the White House kitchen could provide, since it ordered them from an outside bakery.

"The body was not in the linen closet on the third floor on Friday morning. That we know. It is all but impossible, is it not, Mr. Baines, that the body was moved to the third floor during the day on Friday?"

"I would think that's as impossible a thing as impossible can be," said Baines.

"Which means that the body was moved Friday night," said Mrs. Roosevelt.

"Saturday or Sunday nights are not impossible."

"Granted. Movement during the day—"

"Is all but impossible."

"And movement at night," she said, "is all but impossible except for someone intimately acquainted with the White House—which returns to my original point."

"Whoever it was, he has to have been all over the place," said Baines.

"More than once, to have some idea how the place is guarded."

"Let us go back to Thursday, the day when Lucinda was killed."

"Security in the White House was tighter that day than it has been any other day since I've worked here," said Baines. "And it was on Friday."

"Until?"

"Until the royals were gone. Then everyone heaved a sigh of relief and . . . Yeah. I see your point."

"Even so," she said, "it would have been all but impossible for someone to carry a body from the ground floor to the third floor. Consider the risk, as well. I can see only two possibilities: first, that she was somehow induced to go up to the third floor and was killed there, or, second, that her body was somehow hoisted up an elevator shaft or even up the outside of the building. The second idea seems fantastic, but it does explain the rope marks in her armpits."

"Let's go look," said Baines.

A few minutes later they stood on the promenade that all but encircled the third floor of the White House. It was surrounded by a marble balustrade. Behind the rather narrow promenade, windows and doors opened into third-floor apartments and rooms.

"Fantastic as the idea seems," said Mrs. Roosevelt, "it is possible, you see, that the body was hoisted up here by rope."

"By a strong man," said Baines.

"You are suggesting that eliminates David Lasky," said the First Lady. "If we accept so fanciful a notion as that she was hauled up here with a rope, why exclude from our fancy the possibility that the murderer used a set of pulleys?"

Baines shook his head. "This gets less and less likely."

"All right," said Mrs. Roosevelt. "But let's just carry it through. Lucinda's body was hidden somewhere below: maybe in one of the cabinets in the room where they are working on the Wilson archives. We both noticed that those cabinets are large enough to hide a body. What is more, for two days the archives staff was working as maids and an usher—meaning that they were out of sight. The murderer returns to the White House on Friday night and uses a rope to raise the body from the ground to the balustrade, hauls it over, and takes it in through any one of these doors and windows. He hides it in the linen closet and departs. I acknowledge that it seems an unlikely scenario, but is it impossible?"

Baines leaned over the balustrade and looked down. They were on the east end of the White House. "The floodlights are turned off at midnight to save electricity," he said. "Even while they are on, they light the north and south facades, not so much the east and west ends. Your fantasy is possible."

Mrs. Roosevelt nodded. "I thought so."

"Except for another difficulty with it," said Baines. "*Why?* Why would someone kill Lucinda Robinson on the ground floor, then haul her body all the way up here and hide it in a closet where it was bound to be discovered no later than Monday?"

"I should like to know," said Mrs. Roosevelt.

Ed Kennelly arrived at the White House. He had checked police records, looking for the names Charles Pitt and Fred Schoenberg—men mentioned by Mary Logan as having dated Lucinda Robinson.

"I also checked the name Chester Horlick, the one Mary said was *her* date. None of them have police records. The city directory has an entry for Horlick and Schoenberg, none for Pitt. Horlick is the owner of a shoe store. Schoenberg is assistant manager of a wholesale grocery business. Schoenberg . . . Well, I called on our new friend Brother Willoughby. He knew who Charles Pitt is. He's the younger of the two sons of Congressman William Pitt."

"So," said Mrs. Roosevelt. "If Lucinda dated *him* and became intimate, she could well talk about marrying wealth and position. I didn't think of the congressman's son when Mary Logan mentioned the name Pitt."

"The story from Willoughby is that Pitt is something of a spoiled brat," said Kennelly.

"His father," said the First Lady, "is a congressman from North Carolina. The Pitt family, which is, I understand, very distantly related to the two British prime ministers with the name William Pitt, made an immense fortune in the tobacco business, rivaling the Duke family in that regard. The Pitt children are all very polished."

"The question is, then, do we call these fellows in and interrogate them? I sorta think we got to."

"I suggest that I invite Charles Pitt here and talk to him myself," said Mrs. Roosevelt. "His being the son of Congressman Pitt makes the situation just a bit delicate."

"I'll talk to the others," said Kennelly.

* * *

When Kennelly walked into Horlick's Shoe Store on Eye Street and asked to see Chester Horlick, a clerk pointed to a man sitting on a shoe salesman's stool in front of a customer and showing her a variety of shoes. Kennelly had to wait a quarter of an hour before the woman left—without buying anything.

"Captain . . . Kennelly? Yes, Sir. What can I do for you?"

"I'd like to talk to you about Lucinda Robinson."

Horlick frowned, then nodded. He pointed to one of the chairs where customers sat while they were fitted with shoes and said, "Have a seat." He sat down in the next chair.

Kennelly had observed already that Horlick was a small man, hardly the man likely to have carried a body up through the White House—or even to have hauled it up with a rope. He wore silver-rimmed glasses astride a long, narrow nose, and he had a pointed chin. His fleshy lower lip extended beyond his upper lip. His face was freckled, also pitted a bit, presumably by acne. He wore a cream-white, summer-weight, double-breasted suit and tan shoes.

Kennelly reached to one of the smoking stands that stood handy in the shoe store and crushed out a Lucky. "Why don't we make this simple? Tell me what you know about her."

"I don't know very much, Captain. I was in her company only three times. Double dates, arranged by my friend Dave Lasky. Dave did me a great favor, frankly. The girl he arranged for me was much more attractive than Lucinda Robinson."

"But Lasky was very much taken with Lucinda," said Kennelly. "Right?"

"Yes, he was."

"Why?"

"In the first place, Lucy was a shiksa. You know what that is? A girl who is not Jewish. That's what he wanted to take home to his father: a shiksa. Besides, she was intelligent, well-read, articulate. He knew his father would appreciate that, too. Also, Lucy was . . . How shall I say it?"

"Someone said she was a nymphomaniac."

Horlick shook his head. "I certainly wouldn't say that. But she was affectionate and demonstrative and . . . I am quite certain she accepted Dave as a sexual partner. That doesn't make her a nymphomaniac."

"I hear she made a play for you."

Horlick raised his chin. "You used the right word. 'Play.' She was playful."

"Did you know that Lasky wrote her letters in which he threatened to kill her if she betrayed him?"

"I didn't know that, of course. If it's true, I know Dave was in love with her, and I know he was jealous."

"Do you know who Lasky's father is?"

"Only that he's a businessman in Florida. A success, I understand. Dave had money beyond his government salary."

"Do you know that Lasky has disappeared?"

"I know that he's not answering his phone."

"He's a suspect in the death of Lucinda Robinson."

Horlick sighed. "I guessed that."

"Who did he have to be jealous of?" asked Kennelly.

Chester Horlick glanced around the store, where his clerks were staring at the close conversation between the owner and a D.C. police captain. "Captain," he said. "I have to tell you what I surmise. I couldn't testify to what I'm about to say. I don't have the facts. I'm just guessing."

"I understand."

"Lucy loved men. She loved . . . She loved sex. But she loved something else more. Ambition. Money, luxury, comfort. She was determined to marry well. Dave Lasky had money and a certain social position. She dumped another man, maybe two other men, when she started going out with him. And when she saw something better than Dave, she dumped *him*."

"Who was better than Lasky?"

"Charles Pitt."

"But when Lasky threatened to kill her, he wrote about somebody he called 'the Kraut.' He said 'the Kraut' was an evil man. That can't be Pitt, can it?"

"I heard her mention a German just once. She didn't call him 'the Kraut.' She said something to the effect that she had met the most wonderful man: a German aristocrat, fabulously wealthy. That would have impressed Lucy. Her family was German. She spoke German."

"Robinson is not a German name," said Kennelly.

"Rotkehlchen," said Horlick. "Whatta you want to bet?"

"Anyway, this German . . ."

"It made Dave jealous then and there. The German was a wonderful man, she said."

"Wealthy . . ."

"So she said."

"A German, not a German-American."

"So she said."

"If you hear from Lasky, let me know," said Kennelly.

Horlick closed his eyes for a moment, then nodded sadly.

"I appreciate your coming on such short notice, Mr. Pitt," said the First Lady. "Would you prefer tea or coffee?"

"Uh . . . tea please," said Charles Pitt.

"With sugar? Cream?"

"Lemon."

Mrs. Roosevelt poured. The teapot sat on a silver tray believed to have been part of a White House tea service since the days of James and Dolley Madison. If it was, it was the only item left from that tea service. Very little of the furnishings of the White House dated back so far. Various later presidents had furnished the White House to their tastes, transferring older furniture to warehouses, selling much of it. President Chester Allen Arthur had sold twenty-four wagonloads of White House furnishings at auction to make space in its rooms for the Gilded Age gimcracks he preferred. Because she had never been in there, Mrs. Roosevelt did not know that exquisite marble busts of Washington and Jackson languished on shelves in the ground floor men's room. The cups and saucers of the tea service came from Hyde Park.

"As I say, it is good of you to come on short notice."

"Any notice at all is sufficient when one is invited to take tea with the First Lady at the White House," said Charles Pitt.

"Have you any idea why I asked you to come?" she asked.

"I shall guess it is because you want to ask me something about Lucy Robinson."

Though it was almost summer in Washington, Charles Pitt wore wool: a crisply pressed gray, two-piece, single-breasted suit, with a white shirt and a regimental-stripe necktie. His black shoes shone. He sat with long-practiced grace and confidence, holding his cup and saucer steady. His eyes were blue and a little bulgy and heavy-lidded: the only deviation from otherwise very regular features. He had a neatly trimmed mustache, a little too thick to be called a pencil mustache. He was in his forties, Mrs. Roosevelt knew, and so was by far the oldest man who had dated Lucinda Robinson.

"You've been in the White House many times, I believe, Mr. Pitt," said Mrs. Roosevelt.

Pitt grinned. "Ma'am," he said, "my father brought me to Washington when I was a lad, during the presidency of William Howard Taft. I grew up in Washington and have had many occasions to visit the White House. In fact, I came here as a young man to see Margaret Wilson. I need hardly tell you that the Wilson girls led me on a merry chase through every part of the house. They used to have treasure hunts, going into every closet and drawer in the house, finding things and speculating about whose they might once have been. They found a pair of eyeglasses that looked a hundred years old and decided after a while that they had belonged to Abraham Lincoln. They were almost right. Examination by the curators of the Smithsonian established them as having been worn by Edwin M. Stanton and left behind in a bureau drawer for fifty years."

"They were sprightly young women, as I recall."

"Sprightly? I should say they were sprightly! Margaret used to join one of the tour groups being led through the White House, and as they were going through, she would talk loudly about what a terrible president Woodrow Wilson was. The scandalized tourists never guessed she was President Wilson's daughter."

"I assume you are aware of the circumstances of Lucinda Robinson's death."

"Yes. I read about it. It's a tragic thing."

"We have been told that you dated Lucinda."

"Yes. I certainly did."

"Mr. Pitt, I am trying to help the police and Secret Service to identify the person who murdered Lucinda. I have, in my small way, helped them in one or two matters before. The circumstances require me to ask you questions I would not otherwise ask. Please do understand."

"I believe you are doing me a favor," said Pitt. "We shall discuss my relationship with Lucy over tea. Otherwise, I should probably have to discuss it with some rude and burly detective at police headquarters."

"The detective in charge of the case, Captain Edward Kennelly, is not rude or burly, but he is direct. He is in fact blunt."

"I should rather discuss the matter with you," said Pitt.

"Very well. Why don't you just tell me, in narrative form, what sort of relationship you had with Lucinda Robinson?"

"I became aware of her in . . . I believe it was December. I saw her at a party at a home in Georgetown. Now that I think of it, there was a Christmas tree up in the house, so it *was* December. You realize of course that she was not an exceptionally attractive girl. But there was something about her . . . *joie de vivre* that seemed genuine, unaffected. I took notice of her and remembered her. I next saw her here, in the White House. My father is sponsor of a bill relating to an import tax on Egyptian tobacco, and he asked me to deliver a package of amendments to Harry Hopkins. I came in through the East Wing, and as I was walking through the ground-floor hall on my way to the West Wing, I encountered Lucy. We stopped and chatted, and once again I was fascinated by her personality. I asked her if she'd like to have dinner. She accepted my invitation, we went to dinner that evening, and after that I saw her quite often, for several months."

"Did you realize you were not the only young man she was seeing?"

"Yes. She made that clear."

"Did you know any of the other young men she was seeing?"

"No. I never met any of them. I know the name of one: David Lasky, who is a lawyer here in the White House. There was another one who was in business in some small way. I don't mean to be snobbish, but please understand that when I escorted Lucy I took her places where David Lasky or a small businessman were not likely to go. I mean, I took her to the places *I* frequent: private clubs, the homes of friends, and so on."

"You say you saw her for several months. Am I to understand you had stopped seeing her at the time of her death?"

"I hadn't seen her for three or four weeks before she was murdered," said Pitt.

"Was there some reason?"

"Yes. We had a quarrel. Let me see. Maybe I can fix the date." He took out his wallet and pulled from it a tiny calendar. "It was on a Saturday night. I am going to say May thirteenth, though it may have been May sixth. After the quarrel I tried several times to call her. She wouldn't talk to me."

"What was the quarrel about, Mr. Pitt?"

"She told me she was pregnant. She said the baby was mine." He sighed. "Frankly, Mrs. Roosevelt, I had to be skeptical of that. In the first place, I had always taken precautions." He frowned and shook his head. "I am sorry the conversation has to take this turn."

"I am a wife and mother, Mr. Pitt. I am not embarrassed by the facts of life."

"Well . . . I had always taken precautions. Besides—" He sighed again, audibly. "Mrs. Roosevelt, I hope you can understand that a man in my position—I mean, heir to a major share of a family fortune—is compelled to be suspicious when a girl tells him he has made her pregnant. I had to be particularly suspicious when she told me she had confided in Mary Logan—that is, told Mary Logan she was pregnant and that I was responsible. I had to wonder if she hadn't simply decided to attribute her pregnancy to the wealthiest of her lovers."

"Did she propose you marry?" asked the First Lady.

"No. She proposed I make a settlement of money."

"Did *you* propose you marry?"

Pitt shook his head. "No. Oh, I don't say I wouldn't have. If I could have been sure her baby was mine, *certainly* I would have married her. But my enthusiasm for her had subsided somewhat by then."

"Why?"

He ran his fingers over his forehead as if he were developing a headache. "I had concluded . . . reluctantly . . . that she was not the sort of young woman I could introduce to my father, or indeed to any of my family. Her exuberance was charming, but— I hate to slander her, but the fact was, Mrs. Roosevelt, Lucy was *coarse*. Her physical appetites, which were fascinating at first, cloyed in time. She offended some of my friends by the crude things she said, and I stopped taking her to their homes."

"Frankly, that's hard to believe, Mr. Pitt. It seems so out of character for Lucinda."

"She was playful about it. She spoke German. I didn't know what she was saying. One day a friend telephoned me. He asked me if I knew what she had said in his living room the evening before. I had to say I didn't. He told me she had referred to my male organ. She said it was quite ordinary, but she knew a man who had one that was extraordinary. My friend said he supposed she assumed none of the people who heard her understood German. But *he* did, and so did his wife; and his wife said she didn't ever want to see Lucy in her home again. I have never been so embarrassed. I am embarrassed still."

"We have heard something of the kind about her before," said Mrs. Roosevelt gently.

"But I do have to wonder," he said soberly, "if a child of mine didn't die when she died."

"Mr. Pitt, Lucinda Robinson was not pregnant," said the First Lady somberly.

"*What?*"

"The medical examiner did not perform a complete autopsy. But he did examine her to see if she had been sexually abused and to determine if she was pregnant. Unwanted pregnancy is sometimes a motive in the death of a woman. Lucinda was not pregnant."

"Then she was . . . an . . . *unethical adventuress!*"

"It has begun to appear so," said Mrs. Roosevelt. "Let me turn to something else. Did she ever refer to a man as 'the Kraut'?"

He shook his head slowly. "No. 'The Kraut.' No, she never used that term."

"Were you aware that she was also dating a German-speaking man?"

"I . . . That's interesting. My friend who told me his wife would never allow Lucy in their home again, because of the vulgarities she spoke in German, called me about two weeks ago to say he had seen Lucy at a cocktail reception at the German Embassy."

"Your friend is . . . ?"

"An importer of Leica and Rollei cameras. He is much concerned Germany will go to war and his supply of German cameras will be cut off. He remarked to me on the telephone that it was odd to see a young woman who works in the White House at a party at the German Embassy, in view of the tense state of our relations with Germany. I told him she was in no policy-making position, not even in a position near the policy makers."

"Was she with someone at this party?"

"Well, he supposed so, but he couldn't identify anyone. She seemed to be at home and well acquainted. She spoke German—none of her vulgarisms in that crowd. She seemed, he said, exceptionally anxious to make a favorable impression."

"He knows the White House very well," said Mrs. Roosevelt to Ed Kennelly and Jerry Baines. "He had a motive. He thought she might be carrying his child, and she had demanded money from him."

She laid on the table before her the note she had scribbled. Wrote some new words on it.

WHEN
After 10:15

WHERE
?
Ground floor

WHY
???
Pregnancy?

WHY WAS THE BODY
MOVED?

"And he is a big enough man to have done it," she added.

"At least it gives us another reasonably likely suspect," said Baines.

"When all is said and done, Lasky is still the most likely," said Kennelly. "And I think I know where to find him. At least I've got an idea."

"We can use an idea on that subject," said Mrs. Roosevelt. "He has not called again."

Kennelly nodded. "Sam Lasky runs a carpet joint in Florida. It looks straight, within limits. But there are a lot of other carpet joints, here, there, and the other place, and there's some linkage among them. They run different ways, different rules, but the guys in that business know each other."

"Which is why Mr. Joe E. Lewis always has work," said Mrs. Roosevelt.

"Exactly," said Kennelly. "Sam Lasky is not mixed up with, say, Bugsy Siegel; but if Bugsy asks Sam a favor, he gets it."

"Which has what to do with finding David Lasky?" asked Baines.

"It's a little complicated," said Kennelly. "It took some checking. Okay. Sam Lasky is from New York. He ran a gambling casino at Saratoga Springs, in partnership with several other men, including Frank Costello. Frank Costello got out of the Saratoga Springs place. So did Sam Lasky. Don't ask me why. But the place in Saratoga Springs still rents slot machines from . . . guess who? Frank Costello. Costello runs a business in Texas, making and renting slots. The place was raided lately. The customer list was seized. Listed as renting slot machines from Costello is . . . guess who? Sam Lasky. Okay, so no big deal. The Florida authorities don't care. *But* guess who else rents slots from Costello? Carmine Plumeri. And who is Carmine Plumeri?"

"Really, Ed!" protested Baines.

"Carmine Plumeri," said Kennelly, "owns Dolly's, the joint across the river in Virginia. Remember the book of matches we found in Lasky's drawer? From Dolly's. I don't think it's such a long shot that Carmine Plumeri is doing Sam Lasky a favor and hiding his son."

"You have done a lot of careful investigatory work," said Mrs. Roosevelt.

"A few calls, a few questions," said Kennelly. "Just an odd lead I thought might be worth following." He shrugged. "I could be one hundred per cent wrong."

"Are you planning on going out there this evening?"

"I think I'll try it."

Mrs. Roosevelt smiled slyly. "Maybe Detective Broderick should go, too."

"Ma'am—"

"Oh, I think Detective Broderick should assist in the apprehension of Mr. Lasky. You will be outside your jurisdiction, and Martha Broderick's persuasive powers might prove effective."

Joe Kennedy knew how to please President Roosevelt. He had flown from London to New York on the Clipper, then hurried down to Washington, carrying in his valise four wrapped bottles of single-malt Scotch. He brought them to the President's cocktail hour, and now they were sipping: Scotch, neat, no water, no ice.

"How's the family, Joe?"

"Just fine, Frank," said Kennedy. "Jack will be going back to London with me. You know, he was aboard the *Normandie* with Eleanor last fall during the Munich crisis. He was on his way back for his Harvard school year . . . feeling bad, rather sick."

"Babs didn't tell me the boy was sick."

The President and Ambassador Kennedy were alone. Even Missy had not yet arrived. Kennedy grinned and said, "Actually, he wasn't so much sick as in pain. You see, Jack was *circumcised* last fall, and that's a painful operation for a young man his age."

"How old is Jack?"

"He was twenty-one at the time. He's twenty-two now. He'd begun to wonder if he'd ever be able to use the thing again."

"He has recovered, I hope," said the President.

"More than I could have wished," said Joe Kennedy.

The President laughed. "What do you think of what's going on in Moscow, Joe?"

"Frank . . . Hitler is going to take over the Balkans. And there's nothing we can do about it."

"The British, the French, and the Russians," said the President. "What can they do about it?"

"I suppose the Soviet Union could fight," said Kennedy. "But Hitler has a far greater army now than he had at the time of Munich. He'll beat the Russians."

"Will he if the British and French attack him in the west?"

Kennedy nodded grimly. "Hitler will hold the French army out of Germany, fighting behind his West Wall, which is now complete. The German army is shut out of France by the Maginot Line, and the French army is shut out of Germany by the West Wall. Hitler has always talked about the *Lebensraum*—living room—Germany needed in the east. He'll take it, and there's nothing anyone can do about it."

"What happens to Europe? What happens to the world?"

"One of two things will happen, I believe," said Ambassador Kennedy. "Germany will take over Hungary and Romania, Yugoslavia, and maybe even Greece. With all of that, it will be restored to even greater prestige and prosperity than it had in 1914, and the Germans will be proud and content. Or, having swallowed all those countries, Germany will die of indigestion."

"It's not a very hopeful prospect, is it, Joe?"

"I'm a businessman, Frank. In my belief, when the Germans are making comfortable profits they will cease to be aggressive."

VIII

The carpet joint called Dolly's was located on Sleepy Hollow Road in Fairfax County. Ed Kennelly said there was no point in arriving there much before nine o'clock, since nothing much would happen there before nine—especially on a Friday night. Jerry Baines insisted that the First Lady could not venture into such a place without Secret Service protection, so he was with her and Kennelly.

Four of them went to Dolly's. The fourth was a younger Secret Service agent named Dominic Deconcini. He was an exceptionally handsome young man: features sharp and fine, complexion swarthy, eyes dark and penetrating, a noncommittal, noncommunicative smile fixed on his face. He carried a .38 caliber Colt revolver in a shoulder holster under his left arm.

The Secret Service had also provided an undercover car: a 1937 LaSalle with Virginia license plates.

No sign indicated where Dolly's was. Customers had to *know* where it was. It was some fifty yards off the road, invisible within a piney wood. Kennelly, who had been thoroughly briefed as to how to find it, drove past the turnoff once and had to turn around and come back.

The wood, which shielded the roadhouse from view even in winter, was redolent with the odor of fresh pine needles and old needles rotting on the ground. It was a pleasant atmosphere—somehow reassuring. The road made two turns and then debouched onto a large clearing where the roadhouse stood.

From outside, Dolly's was anything but prepossessing. It was dark outside, a sprawling one-story frame building that had the aspect of a warehouse. All that suggested it was anything else was the number of cars parked in the clearing.

The cars themselves suggested something. Few of them were Plymouths, Fords, and Chevrolets. Most of them were Cadillacs, Packards, LaSalles, Buicks, and Chryslers.

An attendant with a flashlight swept his beam to indicate where Deconcini should park, then came up beside the car and asked who the people in the car were.

"Haven't been here before," said Kennelly. "Congressman Bailey said to use his name."

"It'll be ten dollars apiece to join the club," said the attendant.

"Fine."

The attendant swung the beam of his flashlight to the door. "Right over there," he said. "Knock three times."

Inside, the unprepossessing warehouse turned out to be an elegant nightclub: a dining room with stage, where an orchestra played, a casino, and private rooms out of sight that might hold anything. The décor was dominated by maroon plush and gold braid, something like the interior of a 1920s movie palace. Statues—mostly cherubs, but more dominantly images of Venus and Bacchus—were obviously molded of gilded plaster. The naked figures in the small fountains had been cast of something more water-resistant than plaster but were not marble or bronze.

Kennelly, Baines, and Deconcini hovered around the First

Lady as they stood first at a desk and became members of the club. She had come to enjoy her role as Detective Broderick and assumed it was the sharp eye of an FBI agent that had revealed her identity to Willoughby—that plus the fact that he had seen her in both personae in one day. As a member of Dolly's, she was Mrs. Edward Gruber—that is, Mrs. Ed Kennelly.

"Would you care to dine or to try your luck at one of the tables?" a maître d' asked.

"I want to play, but I want to eat first," said Kennelly.

The maître d' bowed and led them to a table in the dining room. It was a table to the side, out of the stage lights—which suited this party just fine.

"Champagne?"

"I think we'd rather have a bottle of Scotch," said Kennelly firmly.

As her eyes became accustomed to the low light at the dining tables, Mrs. Roosevelt remarked to Ed Kennelly that she was glad she was there as Martha Broderick. "I know too many people here," she said.

"This is not a low joint," said Kennelly. "I wouldn't have brought you here if it was."

"Even so, it's illegal," she said. "Gambling . . . Liquor after hours. And so on."

"It was a speakeasy," said Baines. "One of the most successful in the Washington area."

The First Lady nodded toward a table across the room. "The tall man is Congressman Lyndon Johnson, one of the up-and-coming young men in the new Congress. From Texas. A protégé of Sam Rayburn. The man with him is, I think, a new congressman from Arkansas named Wilbur Mills."

"I don't think the place will be raided tonight," said Deconcini. "Unless I am mistaken, the two gentlemen over there are Chief Justice Charles Evans Hughes and Justice Louis Brandeis."

"My word!" said Mrs. Roosevelt. "The other man with them is the Attorney General!"

Kennelly laughed.

"I really didn't know," she said, "that such gentlemen frequented . . . carpet joints."

Baines joined Kennelly in laughing. "Ma'am," he said. "I'm afraid the world is a somewhat different place than you suppose."

"There are carpet joints and carpet joints," said Kennelly. "Look around. You don't see Martin Dies . . . Everett Dirksen . . ."

"I'll tell you something interesting," said Kennelly. "Huey Long couldn't get in here. They turned him away at the door. Called him a hoodlum."

Mrs. Roosevelt lifted her eyebrows. "Do you mean there is a hierarchy of elegance and exclusivity among such places?"

Kennelly frowned and hesitated for a moment, as if he did not entirely understand the words she had used. Then he nodded and said, "Definitely. It was that way with speakeasies. Some of them, you had to be somebody to get in."

The orchestra stopped playing, and the musicians began moving their chairs, music stands, and instruments to the floor just in front of the stage. A waiter brought the Scotch to the table. The First Lady held a cautioning hand over her glass, signaling to Kennelly that he was to pour only a taste for her. She rarely drank spirits. They had a disconcerting effect on her.

With the orchestra seated below the stage, bright spotlights illuminated it, and a pretty young girl came out to dance. Dressed in a pink satin costume, she strode back and forth across the stage, while the orchestra blared a tune with a strong rhythm.

The waiter had also left a card: the menu. Diners had little choice. Shrimp cocktail was apparently not optional; it came with every dinner. After that the choice was steak or chicken. There were no prices on the menu, except for the wines and liquors listed on the reverse side.

"I was told to order steak," said Kennelly.

Mrs. Roosevelt put the menu down. She took a cautious sip of the whisky. The dancer on the stage had pulled off her evening gloves and tossed them aside. Now she was opening the hooks that closed her pink satin vest.

"Uh . . . Are we about to witness what is called a strip-tease?" the First Lady asked Kennelly.

"Yeah, I'm afraid we are. Sorry, Ma'am."

"Oh, don't be afraid or sorry. It wouldn't do for the First Lady to attend such a performance, I suppose, but nothing prevents Detective Broderick from seeing it . . . and satisfying a longstanding curiosity."

The dancer removed the vest and continued to dance wearing nothing above her waist but a flimsy halter, also of pink satin.

A young man walked across the dining room, not led by a maître d', and took a table three tables away from the one where Mrs. Roosevelt sat and did not notice him. Baines did, though. He looked away from the stage and peered at the young man.

"Bingo . . ." he muttered to the First Lady, nodding toward the young man.

Mrs. Roosevelt glanced at the young man. He was David Lasky.

Deconcini was staring at Lasky. He had seen him at the White House and could identify him, too. "Don't stare," said Baines. "We don't want him to recognize us."

A waiter put a bottle of whisky before Lasky. It was half empty. "Eats here every night, I bet," commented Kennelly.

"My word," said Mrs. Roosevelt as the dancer bent over and pulled down two long zippers that slit her skirt from her waist to her ankles, exposing bare hips and legs. "How far will she go?" she whispered to Kennelly.

Ed Kennelly grinned and shrugged.

It was obvious that the dancer wasn't finished yet. She began toying with her halter, as if she were going to take it off. Some in the crowd applauded, to encourage her. Mrs. Roosevelt noticed that David Lasky seemed to be paying hardly any attention to the girl. She surmised that he had seen the performance too many times before.

"We shall have to decide what we are going to do," said Mrs. Roosevelt. "Shall we approach him?"

"We must preserve your anonymity," said Baines. "We must not make a scene."

"I have to agree. Well . . . At least we know where he is."

"We can snatch him out of here in the daytime, if we want to," said Kennelly. "I've got no jurisdiction out here, but you two have. You could make a Secret Service arrest."

"Let's consider the possibility of approaching him quietly and telling him he will have to submit to interrogation," said Mrs. Roosevelt. "I see no reason why that should create a scene."

Mrs. Roosevelt used her right hand to cover her amazed smile as the dancer pulled off her halter and exposed her breasts.

Their waiter returned and asked if they wanted to order their dinner. All ordered steaks. Mrs. Roosevelt asked for hers well done. The others ordered theirs rare. She sipped a bit more of her whisky, and Kennelly poured more into her glass.

The girl on the stage was now dancing with her breasts bare and, to Mrs. Roosevelt's amazement, began to toy with her skirt as if she were going to take it off, too. Indeed, after a moment she did.

"Is that what is called a G-string?" the First Lady asked Kennelly.

"That's what it's called."

"Is this what they do at the Gayety Burlesque, in Washington?"

"Yes, but they don't go as far. Since this is a private club, she may—"

She did, then quickly trotted off stage, to enthusiastic applause.

"Is everything okay? Are you enjoying yourselves, folks?"

They looked up. A small man, maybe sixty years old, wearing a tuxedo, had come to their table. He had a swarthy complexion and a wrinkled face, a high forehead from which his hair had receded, wrinkly eyes, and a dark mustache.

"I'm Carmine Plumeri. I'm the owner. Would you mind if I pull up a chair and join you for a minute?"

"Please do," said Baines.

Plumeri pulled a chair away from an adjoining table and sat down. A waiter was waiting for his signal, and Plumeri beckoned him over and said, "Champagne. Two bottles. It's on the house, of course."

"Well, thank you," said Baines.

Carmine Plumeri used his thumbnail to scratch the side of his nose. He spoke to Kennelly. "Unless I'm wrong, and I don't think I am, you're Captain Edward Kennelly of the District police. That would make the rest of you police, too—or maybe Secret Service. Hmm?"

"You got me," said Kennelly. "I'd like to know how."

Plumeri spoke dryly, without a smile, in a flat voice. "I have a better question. How'd you know to come looking here? That's the real question, but I don't suppose you'll give me an answer."

"It was an educated guess," said Kennelly.

"Yeah. Well, so was me figuring you out. When you're in my line of business—and have been in my line as long as I have—you develop certain instincts. It goes with the job. Just like certain instincts go with your job, Captain, and helped you make your educated guess. You want to know specifically how I figured you out?"

"Yeah," said Kennelly. "Maybe I should have come in a wig and a false beard."

Plumeri did not react to the essay at humor. "You're new. It's the first time you were ever here. The parking lot guy gave the guy at the door the high sign. From that point, a whole lot of guys that work here made a point of taking a look at you. I hire guys from Washington, mostly. Pretty soon one of them says, 'Yeah. I know this guy.' Y' see? Nothing complicated."

"Okay. You know why I'm here?" Kennelly asked.

Plumeri nodded. "Something else. I'm afraid to even guess who the lady is. But don't worry about it. Have a good time. Everything's on me, including the forty dollars you paid to get in. Now . . . You want to talk to Dave, right?"

"Right."

"I'm gonna tell him to talk to you. If he gets up and runs out the door, I won't try to stop him. And don't you. You have no jurisdiction here, Kennelly. Besides, we don't want the lady's real name to come out. But . . . . don't worry. Dave's a sensible young guy. He'll talk to you. I'm gonna go sit down with him now. Enjoy your dinner. Enjoy the show. Afterwards, I'll arrange for you and Dave to meet in a private room."

Carmine Plumeri slid his chair back and got up. He went over and sat down with Lasky, and they could see the two of them in solemn conversation.

A second stripteaser repeated the performance of the first. This one was a little older, a little heavier, and somehow, through some skill or instinct, a little more erotic. Although she was not as fresh or attractive—in Mrs. Roosevelt's judgment—she won more applause.

She was followed to the stage by a near-legendary per-
former. The orchestra played a fanfare, an announcer carried
a stand microphone to the center of the stage, and he introduced her—

"Ladies and gentlemen! The one, the only, the fabu-
lous . . . *the last of the red-hot mamas!* SOPHIE TUCKER!"

The heavy-set, blowzy bleached blonde flounced to the
center of the stage and delivered one of her signature lines—

"I'll never forget it!"

Then she launched into an off-color story about the relationship she said she'd once had with an Indian chief.

For nearly an hour Sophie Tucker held her audience, entertaining them with risqué lines and blue stories, some of
them combined with cogent commentary on contemporary
manners and morals. She sang. She danced. She lifted her
skirts and showed her plump legs. Once she bent over, and
one of her huge breasts fell from her dress. She pretended
she was surprised and shocked and shoved it back in immediately.

"That one's incorrigible," she explained. "A fresh-air fiend,
always trying to get outside and breathe."

Mrs. Roosevelt had never seen or heard any such performance in her life and had not guessed that any such performance was judged entertaining by many, many Americans. At
first she stiffened with shock and disapproval. After a while
she decided that since she was here she might as well make
the most of the occasion. She could not understand half of
what the gross woman said, but from time to time she heard
a witty comment about something that was within her ken
and experience, and could not help but laugh. She realized
that if she hadn't, looking around at her own table and all the
rest of the dining room, she would probably have been alone.
She decided the performance was an experience worth
having—once—and she relaxed, tried to follow the mono-

logue, tried to understand, and from time to time found herself genuinely amused.

"He had a male paart . . . that he *called* a dong . . .
s' long . . . like King Kong . . . Why, he could've *used* it . . .
t' bong . . . a *gong. I'll never forget it.*"

The audience guffawed. Mrs. Roosevelt, though she didn't
think that was witty at all, found that she had to laugh, in the
spirit of things. She put the back of her hand to her mouth
and chuckled.

A bucket of ice and their second bottle of champagne, also
their bottle of Scotch, were moved into a private room just
off the dining room. They sat at a round table for eight,
spread with a white linen cloth, with a single yellow rose in a
vase in the center of the table.

David Lasky had been waiting there for them, and Mrs.
Roosevelt tried to seat the group so as not to create the appearance of a confrontation between them and Lasky. She
did not succeed and so sat one chair removed from him herself. She had put aside her turban and wiped off her lipstick,
abandoning her guise as Detective Broderick.

Lasky was a slight young man. His skin had an unhealthy-
looking grayish color. He had a prominent Adam's apple that
bobbed in his throat when he spoke. He wore gold-rimmed
eyeglasses. He must have been unable to shave correctly, because eruptions of a few dark whiskers stood at points on his
cheeks and along his jawline. His demeanor was solemn and
tense, as he demonstrated clearly in the tentative way he
handled his cigarillo. He had a glass before him, and he
needed say only a few words to make it apparent that he'd
had a good deal to drink.

Mrs. Roosevelt was curious to know what had attracted
Lucinda Robinson to this awkward, apprehensive little fellow.

"You can't arrest me," Lasky said. "But you can get the Virginia authorities to do it. Maybe you've already asked them."

"The worst thing that stands against you, Mr. Lasky," said Mrs. Roosevelt, "is your abrupt departure and your hiding out for a week."

"I explained why I don't dare go to jail," said Lasky.

"We can protect you, young fella," said Kennelly.

"I suppose you can. But *would* you have, if I'd asked you to? Would you have taken me seriously?"

"All you'd have had to do was tell me the name of your father," said Kennelly.

"I didn't want my father to know about this."

"Are you tryin' to tell me he *doesn't?* C'mon, Lasky. Your father knows where you are, and why."

"He does now. Mr. Hopkins called him."

"Are you saying your father didn't call Carmine Plumeri and ask him to take you in?"

"He didn't. I'd been coming out here as long as I'd been in Washington. I brought Lucy to Dolly's. Other girls, too. It made quite an impression on them that I was received as an honored guest here. I knew Mr. Plumeri. I could ask him to help me. I didn't have to ask my father to arrange it. And when my father heard from Mr. Hopkins that I was in trouble, naturally he called Mr. Plumeri. He called to find out if Mr. Plumeri knew where I was, not to ask him to take me in."

"You say you are in trouble," said Mrs. Roosevelt. "What trouble are you in, Mr. Lasky? Why did you leave your job and apartment suddenly and hide out in this club?"

"I wrote very foolish letters to Lucy," he said. "I was in a high state of emotion when I wrote them. When I realized she was probably dead, I remembered those letters. I knew she'd saved them; she told me she did. And I knew when you found them you would assume I had killed her. Why not? That's what anyone would assume."

"Let's go back to something," said Kennelly. "When did you last see Lucinda Robinson?"

"Except that I saw her body at the funeral home, the last time I saw her was on Thursday morning of last week. That was the—"

"The eighth," said Kennelly.

"Yes. It was the day when the King and Queen were due to arrive. I'd been told I was welcome to take a place in the entrance hall and see them go by. I went over to Lucy's office to see where she would be. I told her it would be nice if we could see the royal couple together. It would be a memorable experience. I guess I still had the idea that if we shared something memorable it would make her more inclined to . . . to see me again."

"Did you speak with her while she was sitting at her desk?" asked Mrs. Roosevelt.

"No. I asked her to step out in the arcade for a moment. I didn't want to face Mrs. Helm at that moment."

"What did she say?"

"She said she had other plans. She was curt about it."

"And that was the last time you saw her alive?"

"Yes. I went back to my office, feeling bad. Feeling foolish, as a matter of fact."

"What time was that?"

"About ten o'clock, I think."

"You didn't see her in the hall when the King and Queen arrived at the White House?"

"No."

"When did you learn she was dead? And how?"

"I tried to telephone her at the boardinghouse. She wasn't there. I supposed she was out with another man, which troubled me, so I called her again after eleven. She had not come in. The next morning I went over to her desk again. She had not come in. When she didn't show up by noon, I began to imagine horrible things that could have happened to her. When the idea came to my mind that she might be dead—"

"You decided to skedaddle," said Kennelly.

"Until she was found all right or someone else was found to have harmed her."

Baines and Deconcini only listened to the interrogation. The First Lady and Kennelly were enough questioners. But they watched and listened intently, and Baines sipped Scotch and became a little unsteady.

"Mr. Lasky," said Mrs. Roosevelt, "how many men besides yourself dated Lucinda during the time you knew her?"

"When I first met her, she was seeing a man named Grant, an automobile salesman. I confess that I brought her out here to Dolly's, to show her I could do more lavish things for her than Grant could. She stopped seeing Grant. Then there was a man named Schoenberg. She saw him sometimes, but I think not often. Except for those two . . . the Kraut."

"Did you ever hear of a man named Charles Pitt?"

"The son of the congressman? I've heard of him."

"Did you know she dated him, too?"

Lasky shook his head. He reached for the bottle and poured himself another shot of Scotch. "When?" he asked.

"Well, that's of course another question," said Mrs. Roosevelt. "What was the sequence? When did you first meet Lucinda? And where?"

"I met her in the White House. At the Christmas party you and the President held for the staff. That was of course in December."

"When did you sense she had lost interest in you?"

"Within the last two months. That's when she began to see the German, whoever he was. I didn't know about Pitt, though to tell the truth, I should have suspected there was another man somewhere."

"Did she encourage you to think she was in love with you?" asked Mrs. Roosevelt.

"I thought she did."

"She was in fact a very affectionate young woman."

Lasky closed his eyes and nodded. "Very."

Ed Kennelly spoke. "I'm goin' to suggest one of you fellows take Mrs. Roosevelt for a walk for a few minutes. I wanta ask Lasky some personal questions, if you know what I mean."

Deconcini rose. "Mrs. Roosevelt?"

She sighed, then stood. "I must agree this may become so . . . personal I should not hear it," she said.

After the door closed behind the First Lady and Dominic Deconcini, Kennelly sat for a long moment staring at Lasky, glancing at Baines, then staring at Lasky again.

"I'm looking for a motive, Lasky," he said. "The medical examiner says she wasn't sexually abused. I suppose she wasn't. How could a guy rape a woman in the White House in the middle of the morning? She wasn't pregnant, though she told Pitt she was. One witness has called her a nymphomaniac. What about it? What the hell was she?"

"She was the most . . . affectionate girl I've ever known," said David Lasky somberly.

"It was more than that, though, wasn't it?"

"I suppose so."

"You're a stud, aren't you, Lasky? Hung like a horse?"

Lasky hesitated, then shrugged and said, "Your words, not mine, Captain."

"Did you know she teased other guys about not being as big as you? In German. She made fun of Pitt one night at a fancy cocktail party, telling him in German, which he didn't understand, that his wasn't as big as yours. It was a mistake. Their charming hostess understood German, was shocked, and told Pitt never to bring her to the house again."

Lasky shook his head. "She was very bold, very playful," he said.

"She was giving it to you regularly and suddenly cut you off and started giving to somebody else instead, like the Kraut," said Kennelly. "That could make a man mad as hell."

"That's not why I wrote her those letters," said Lasky. "I *loved* her."

"Okay, let's suppose you didn't kill her. But having what she gave and then not getting it anymore could make a man pretty mad, couldn't it?"

Lasky nodded. "I won't deny I longed for what she did for me."

"So maybe it didn't make you mad enough to kill her. But maybe it made somebody else that mad."

"Possible . . ."

"You don't have to go into details, but . . . uh, she *was* a nympho, wasn't she?"

Lasky put a hand to his forehead. "I don't know how you define that word exactly," he said, rubbing his forehead and eyes. "She wasn't really *obsessed* with going to bed. Nights when we came out here to Dolly's, we didn't— But whenever we did, it was . . . unbelievable. She loved it. Loved to give more than to take. I . . . Do I have to tell you what she did?"

"I have a vivid imagination," said Kennelly. "But somebody might really rather see her die than have to think about her taking all that away from him and giving it to somebody else. Right?"

"Maybe. But not me. I really did love her."

"I believe you, kid. You took a hell of a risk coming to that funeral home."

"I had to."

"We can ask Mrs. Roosevelt to come back in. You understand, no one's to know she was here tonight."

"Even Mr. Plumeri doesn't know for sure," said Lasky. "He's guessed, but he can't believe it's true."

Baines returned with the First Lady and Deconcini. They had been standing in a corridor, watching another stripper.

"It would help you," Mrs. Roosevelt said to Lasky, "if you could account for your whereabouts at the time when Lucinda was killed."

"I can't do that. I don't know when she was killed."

"Let us say between ten-fifteen and one o'clock."

"I was in my office most of that time. I spoke with Mr. Hopkins on the phone once. I spoke with my secretary. And finally I did go over to see the King and Queen enter the White House. But . . . What would it have taken me to go across the first floor and murder Lucy? Ten minutes? I don't think I can cover every ten minutes."

"Where were you on Friday night?" asked Mrs. Roosevelt.

"Here," he said.

"Could you have returned to the White House, say after midnight, been there for, say, half an hour, and returned here without anyone here knowing?"

Lasky turned up the palms of his hands. "I suppose so. I have my own car."

"Did you ask her to marry you?" Baines inquired. It was his first question.

"Not in so many words," said Lasky. "I tried to make her understand that I wanted to. At first I thought she was interested. Then I had to conclude she wasn't."

"Gotta be brutal," said Kennelly. "She started with Grant, then went for Schoenberg, then she met you, then went from you to Pitt, then Pitt for the Kraut. Do you see a pattern?"

"Tell me the pattern *you* see."

"Grant's a car salesman. Schoenberg is assistant manager of a wholesale grocery. You're a lawyer and your dad's boy, with more money than a White House lawyer makes. Pitt's rich as hell. Whatta ya wanta bet the Kraut is richer than any of you? She was moving up."

Lasky nodded sadly. "I can see the possibility."

"Guys who find themselves rungs on a ladder don't usually much like it. And ya know what? We may not have found them all yet."

Mrs. Roosevelt sighed and shook her head. "This makes poor Lucinda seem like a very bad young woman."

"Not bad enough to deserve what happened to her," said Kennelly. "Nobody deserves what happened to her."

"No one," Lasky repeated.

"Gonna come back to town?" Kennelly asked.

"To jail?"

"No. But if you try to absquatulate again, I'll sic the FBI on you."

"I probably don't have a job," said Lasky.

"Oh, I think you do," said Mrs. Roosevelt. "You probably had some vacation time coming."

IX

The First Lady dictated two columns early on Saturday morning. She always made a point of giving dictation to Tommy Thompson early on Saturdays, so Tommy could type whatever was dictated and be finished by noon, so she could have her Saturday afternoon off. Most of the White House staff worked five and a half days a week, as did most of the office workers in Washington, government and private.

The second column dealt with what Mrs. Roosevelt thought was an amusing confusion. She had learned from some letters that many people supposed the "Miss Thompson" she often referred to in "My Day" was the newspaperwoman Dorothy Thompson, the wife of Nobel Prize–winning novelist Sinclair Lewis. Some complained that since "Miss Thompson" was so often in the White House, she and her husband must have an inordinate amount of influence on the President. In the column, Mrs. Roosevelt explained that "Miss Thompson" was Malvina Thompson, her secretary, and not Dorothy Thompson. They were laughing about it when the telephone rang.

Tommy answered. "It's Professor Robinson, calling from Minnesota," she said.

Mrs. Roosevelt took the call. "Good morning, Professor. How is it with you and Mrs. Robinson?"

"As well as could be expected!" Like many people, he seemed to suppose that a person should shout into the telephone when making a long-distance call. "It's a very sorry time for us! But we will survive, with God's blessing!"

"I can hear you very clearly, Professor."

"Good," he said, and his voice dropped to a nearly normal level. "Have you learned anything more?"

"I'm afraid not. The police are pursuing several leads, though. Diligently."

"Well, I have been reading over Lucinda's last letters. Looking for clues, you know. There's nothing in her letters that suggests anything to me about who killed her. But you might find something in them, and I'll send them along."

"Good. I will return them after we examine them here."

"I'd like to read you something she wrote. All right?"

"Surely."

"This is dated May 23. It says, 'As you know, I am very happy with my job in the White House. Everyone is so kind. You understand also, though, that I don't want to spend very much time as an assistant social secretary, even if it is to so fine a lady as Mrs. Roosevelt. I now think something very different is going to happen in my life. I won't try to tell you prematurely, because I don't want to disappoint you, but you just may find yourselves before long the parents of a very rich woman with a title of nobility! Working here in the White House has opened wonderful opportunities for me, to meet the very finest people. I have made a point of taking advantage of every one of those contacts, and things are looking very positive for me. More later. Pray with me for the good news!' So . . ." the professor concluded. "What do you make of that?"

"It could be an important clue. A title of nobility . . . We have identified several young men she saw socially, but none have a title. I am sure the investigators will be interested in that."

"I will send the letters along. Thank you for your sympathy and interest."

The only man whose name they had that the First Lady or Kennelly had not interviewed was Fred Schoenberg, identified as the assistant manager of a wholesale grocery supply house.

AUGUST & FRIEDERICH SCHOENBERG & SONS
GROCERIES & SUPPLIES AT WHOLESALE

He was a man with thin sandy hair, a pink complexion, pale blue eyes. He invited Kennelly to sit down with him in his office and offered him a shot of whisky. Kennelly declined, it being midmorning, and Schoenberg poured himself one anyway. He sat in his shirsleeves—sleeves pinched and held back by sleeve garters—and his necktie was a small neat bow of black leather.

"I should have been very pleased," he said to Kennelly in English faintly accented and faintly archaic in wording, "if Lucinda and I could have found a way to overcome our differences and become husband and wife. I was her friend. I considered her my friend until the day she died. I . . . . could not accept her ideas. Let us put the matter more accurately. She could not accept mine."

"Yours being?"

"I am a businessman, Captain Kennelly. With my uncle, I run this business, which was founded by my uncle and father forty years ago. I expect to be here and to retire from this business, forty years from now. This was not the kind of thing Lucinda wished. She had very different ambitions."

"Where did you meet her, Mr. Schoenberg? And how did you become close friends?"

"I met her, Captain, at a meeting of the German-American Bund. You understand, I hope, that the Bund is an organization of Americans of German descent who try to promote amity between our two countries. Captain Kennelly . . . Lucinda's name was Robinson, but before 1917 her father's name was Rotkehlchen, which means robin." He shrugged. "During the Great War, the British royal family changed its name from Saxe-Coburg to Windsor, the Battenbergs changed to Mountbatten, and the Minnesota Rotkehlchens changed to Robinson."

"German-American Bund . . . Do you mean to say Lucinda Robinson was a supporter of Herr Hitler?"

"Only to the extent that she hoped to see improved relations between her family's old country and the United States. Captain Kennelly . . . Adolf Hitler, the Führer, is *a fact.* You cannot say you are a friend of Germany and execrate the leader the German people have elected. I believe Lucinda had reservations about some of the policies of the German government, but she believed that every people has the right to choose its own leaders—and the German people have chosen these."

"Which is your own opinion, too, I imagine," said Kennelly.

Schoenberg tossed back the last of the whisky he had poured for himself. "I am distressed by some of the things Herr Hitler says and does," he said. "On the other hand, family and friends in Germany write to me about how much better life there is, now that the National Socialists are in power. Once a month, on average, I receive a letter from a German Schoenberg, urging me to come back there. I cannot think of it. I was born here. My business is here. The first thing that would happen to me if I went back, I would be called to military service. No, I will not leave this country. And I am no less loyal to it because I have and maintain family contacts in the old country."

"I didn't come to see you to talk politics," said Kennelly.

He paused to light a Lucky. "You say you were still a friend of
Lucinda Robinson's when she died?"

"I was. I considered that I was."

"You had slept with her, I suppose."

"No, sir, I did not!"

"You didn't? You were the only man who knew her who
didn't."

"Nevertheless, I didn't. We were friends. We spoke German together. I talked to her about the possibility of a closer
friendship—meaning marriage ultimately, though I never
used the word. She said we were too different. I came to understand what she meant. She had a wild side. It does not
surprise me to hear you say she slept with men. Even though
we were only friends, she was most demonstrative in her affection. She was, Captain Kennelly . . . How to say it? Lucinda
felt that her life was incomplete. She was looking for something. I don't think she knew just what."

"Did you have dates?"

"We met. I suppose the meetings could be called dates. We
dined together. We went to movies. We went to two more
Bund meetings. We talked."

"Just talked . . ." said Kennelly skeptically.

"Talked," Schoenberg repeated emphatically. "She confided in me."

"What did she confide?"

"She was in many ways a very unhappy young woman,"
said Schoenberg. "She had been conscious all her life that
she was not beautiful. I found her attractive, but I have to
concede she was not beautiful. Her parents had made her to
understand that she was not beautiful and therefore would
have to educate herself well and learn to be pleasant if she
were to find a husband. They let her leave home and come to
Washington, in the hope she would get married here. She had
been rejected by all the eligible young men in her home
town. She was pitifully anxious to please."

"But she was not interested in marrying a businessman like you," Kennelly remarked.

"I think she thought she could do better. She was also seeing a young lawyer. She told me about him. His father owns a nightclub in Florida and does quite well apparently. Then she began to see Charles Pitt. He is very wealthy. I thought she was in love with Charles Pitt. In fact, I'm sure she was."

"But she broke it off with Pitt," said Kennelly. "Why would she do that?"

Schoenberg shook his head. "I don't know. I'm sure she felt he was an opportunity to marry well."

"There was still another man," said Kennelly. "He has been referred to as 'the Kraut.' Who would that have been?"

Schoenberg smiled. "That could have been me," he said.

"Whoever he was, he has been called a dangerous, evil man. Could that have been you?"

"Who has ever called me that? Look at me! I'm a wholesale grocer."

Kennelly had to agree, silently, that the grocer was unprepossessing. He gave the impression of modesty, honesty, and sincerity—the very marks of a wily criminal, in the eyes of a cynical detective.

"Lucinda spoke of another man," said Schoenberg. "She was vague about him, and I have no idea who he was. She changed in the last two months or so. I don't know if it was his influence or—"

"How did she change?"

"It's difficult to say. She became sort of . . . dreamy. One thing— She refused to go to another Bund meeting. I'd thought she enjoyed the meetings: the chance to speak German, to hear reports of things going on in Germany, to chat with people who had visited there recently . . . But the last two times I suggested we might go to a meeting, she adamantly refused."

"What specifically did she say about this other man?"

"Only that she'd met a really extraordinary man and that she was seeing him. I asked her who he was, and she just smiled. I knew it would be pointless to press her."

"No description at all? Nothing that would help me figure out who he is?"

Schoenberg shook his head. "No. Well . . . She said he was a prince. I supposed she meant that figuratively, not literally. I don't think she really meant the man was a prince."

Mrs. Roosevelt left the White House on an official call at noon, chauffeured in a limousine. She had agreed to appear for a few minutes at a "Shirley Temple Look-Alike Contest," being held on The Mall. It was not the sort of thing she usually did, but this was not just a show-business promotion; the proceeds from the sales of food and souvenirs were to be donated to a relief program for the children of West Virginia miners who had been killed in mine accidents.

Wearing a white linen dress with a frilly collar, a pink straw hat, and white gloves, the First Lady climbed from the limousine to the appreciative applause of a large crowd gathered to witness the judging of nearly a hundred little girls whose mothers imagined they somehow resembled Shirley Temple.

She was escorted to the stage and handed the microphone. "I am very glad to be here," she said, "and hope this event will raise a great deal of money for the children of the miners. I hope, too, that at the end of the contest some little girl will be very, very happy. I hope indeed that all the little girls who are enjoying the day will be happy, too."

The master of ceremonies lifted up one of the little girls and introduced her to the First Lady. The child bore no resemblance whatsoever to Shirley temple, except for her frilly short dress and her curled hair. She was a brunette, and when she smiled she showed another difference between herself and Shirley Temple—that she had lost her two front teeth.

"Do you want to be like Shirley Temple, dear?" the master of ceremonies asked.

"Yay-yuss!" said the child with disarming fervor.

"Why?"

"I want to be a big star," she said.

"Or a little star?" suggested Mrs. Roosevelt.

"No, a biiig star! I want to make a lot of money."

"Amelia!" her mother snorted.

Mrs. Roosevelt contributed to the fund by purchasing two Shirley Temple dolls. They would make nice Christmas gifts for two of her granddaughters.

Two young radio announcers asked her to say a few words to their broadcast audiences. She allowed each one in turn to interview her. The first one said his name was John Charles Daly. The second one was Arthur Godfrey.

Early in the afternoon, after the President had eaten lunch at his desk and attended to a few papers, he went upstairs, took off his jacket and tie, and settled down in his shirtsleeves to work on his stamp collection. Stamp collecting had interested him since he was a boy; and because he was denied the pleasures of hunting, fishing, and riding, his collection had become one of his chief pleasures. He looked forward to a drowsy Saturday afternoon.

Even so, he was not unhappy when the phone rang and the receptionist announced that Ambassador Joseph Kennedy was downstairs and would like to see him.

"Back to New York tonight," said Kennedy as soon as he entered the room. "To Boston and the Cape for a couple of days. Then the Clipper back to London. I thought I'd stop in and say good-bye."

The President asked Arthur Prettyman to bring him one of

the bottles of single-malt Scotch the ambassador had given him yesterday. He didn't entrust those bottles to the White House pantry but kept them in his bedroom.

"We talked about Russia and Hungary and Yugoslavia and so on yesterday," said the President. "But we didn't talk about Poland. What do you think about Poland?"

"Hitler will never go to war against Poland," said Kennedy.

"Why not? Because the Polish army is strong. To conquer Poland, Germany would have to take troops from the West Wall, and that would leave it vulnerable to a French invasion, supported by the British. In the end, I think, what Hitler wants most is to overthrow the Communist government in Russia. To do that, he'll want Poland as an ally."

"What of the Polish air force?" the President asked. "Do they have one?"

"There is only one major air force in the world right now, Frank, and that is the German *Luftwaffe*. It's as powerful as all the other European air forces *combined*."

"Including the Russian?"

"I can only rely on Colonel Lindbergh's assessment. He calls the Russian air force negligible."

"So what is going to happen?"

"Hitler is going to absorb Hungary, Rumania, and Yugoslavia—maybe Greece, though I doubt it; that would make too much romantic fuss for very little to gain. Albania will be taken by Mussolini. Poland will look on benignly. Russia will storm and fuss and do nothing, because it can't. Most of the German army will stay in the West Wall, so the French and British will be stymied."

"In the near term, all this," said the President. "What in the long term?"

"Germany will need time to digest all it has swallowed. But when it is ready, it will move on Russia, knock off Stalin's crowd, and annex a large part of the Soviet Union—say, the

Ukraine. Poland will join Hitler and be rewarded with Russian land in the north. The new Europe—say, the Europe of the second half of this century—will be dominated by a vastly stronger Germany, which will lord it over a sharply diminished Russia: Russia under a government that Germany approves. The process that began in the 1860s will reach its culmination. The French and British will grumble but be unable to challenge German domination of the Continent."

"I trust you don't speak so as my ambassador," the President said wryly.

"I do when I'm speaking to *you*," said Kennedy.

The President handed to Kennedy a magnifying glass and pointed to a tiny blue stamp mounted on a album page. Engraved in the center of the three-cent stamp was a picture of a wood-burning locomotive, surrounded by some simple scrollwork.

"Issue of 1869," said the President. "Some of the stamps in this series were the first United States postage stamps showing anything but pictures of American statesmen. Actually, there was one eagle. But others in this series showed a post rider, a steamship, Columbus discovering America, and the signing of the Declaration of Independence. I wouldn't be surprised if it was what got people started to collecting stamps."

"When was the first stamp issued?" Kennedy asked.

"In 1847. Before that, the postmasters just wrote 'Postage paid' and things like that on the envelopes."

"Interesting . . ." said Joe Kennedy.

Back from the Shirley Temple contest, Mrs. Roosevelt sat with Ed Kennelly and Jerry Baines in her office, munching on an apple and sipping iced tea. She stared at her note and added some words to it.

WHEN
After 10:15

WHERE
?
Ground floor

WHY
? ? ?
Pregnancy?
Bund activities? (Unlikely.)

WHY WAS THE BODY
MOVED?

HOW DID THE KILLER GET
IN TO MOVE THE BODY?
(Mr. Pitt's intimate knowledge
of White House.)

WHO IS "THE KRAUT"?

"The final question looms ever larger, doesn't it?" she asked. "Mr. Lasky saw something ominous in the man."

"I don't think he's told us the whole truth yet," said Baines. "By writing her threatening letters, he *made* himself a suspect—which he wouldn't have been otherwise, I'd think."

"He came back to work this morning, incidentally," said Mrs. Roosevelt. "I'd asked Harry to take him back, and Harry did—with reservations."

"Is Pitt a big enough man to have carried the body?" Kennelly asked.

"I should think so, yes," said Mrs. Roosevelt. "He's a husky fellow, in good physical condition. He plays polo."

"Schoenberg thinks she was under some kind of evil influence," said Kennelly. "Or so I gathered. He's an innocent—so innocent that he goes to Bund meetings and still thinks he's a patriotic American. He told me Lucy referred to her new boyfriend—likely meaning the Kraut—as 'a prince.' A prince? Horlick said she told him she was seeing a German aristocrat."

"She wrote to her parents that she might soon marry into a 'title of nobility,' " said Mrs. Roosevelt. "I wonder what that could mean."

"Do you want to call Pitt a suspect?" Kennelly asked.

"I want to call anyone a suspect who might have had anything to do with the crime," said Mrs. Roosevelt. "I'm sorry, Captain Kennelly. That sounds sharp. But this case troubles me more than any other you and I have ever worked on together before. Have you ever had to work with so little information? I can't remember that I ever have. In some cases we've seen too many clues, in this one too few."

Baines left before Kennelly. He was a married man, it was late on Saturday afternoon, and he wanted to go home. Kennelly was in no great hurry. He stayed, and Mrs. Roosevelt ordered up a bottle of bourbon, with ice and soda. She did not drink bourbon, but for this once she poured a little over two ice cubes and poured soda to fill the glass.

"Why don't you light a cigarette?" she said. "I know you smoke. I appreciate it that you don't in my presence, but for now why don't you enjoy a cigarette?"

"Well . . ."

"Go ahead. Please."

Kennelly struck a paper match and lit a Lucky. Mrs. Roosevelt shoved a saucer toward him, suggesting it was for his ashes.

She sighed wearily. "Do you know what is going to happen?" she asked.

"We're going to fail to find out who killed Lucinda Robinson," he answered.

"No. Maybe not. What I'm thinking about is the prospect of war. Ed . . . I have four sons. They will have to go to war. We cannot keep them out, certainly not when other people's sons have to go to war. I am terrified."

"Is it that close?"

She nodded. "Hitler will demand more. He will invade some country. Maybe a Balkan nation. Maybe Poland. Maybe the Netherlands or Belgium. And there will be a major European war. The President has promised and will promise again to keep us out, but that may not be possible. My sons . . . Oh, but what happens to so many other parents' sons?"

Kennelly saw tears on her cheeks. He stood and stepped behind her. He touched the back of her neck. "Ma'am . . ."

"Call me by my name, Ed," she whispered.

"Eleanor . . ."

She reached for his hand and clasped it in her own. "I've said too much," she said in a low and quiet voice. "But you can't always smile, can't always play the optimist."

"Top of the heap is a lonely place . . . ?"

"A cliché, Ed. A terrible cliché."

He used his left hand to stroke the back of her neck. "If you weren't who you are—"

"I know. If I weren't."

She stood, and for a minute they stood facing each other, wordless. Then both of them moved on the same impulse, and Detective Captain Edward Kennelly kissed Mrs. Eleanor Roosevelt.

They separated, smiling at each other, their hands lingering together, then dropping apart. Nothing was possible.

* * *

No one was in the house for the President's cocktail hour. He forewent his shaker and his ice and let Arthur Prettyman help him with his bath and into his pajamas. He sat up against his pillows, glancing over the afternoon newspapers and smoking a cigarette in his holder, reluctant to call for his dinner tray, certain something unappetizing would be brought up from Mrs. Nesbitt's kitchen.

A rap on the door. It opened and Missy came in.

"I thought you'd gone up to New York for the weekend," he said.

She closed the door and turned the night latch. She wore a white peignoir over a white nightgown. "I was, till I looked over the schedule," she said. "Effdee . . . I wouldn't leave you alone on a weekend like this. I think we should have a couple of martinis, then eat, and then maybe we can watch a movie."

The President's spirits rose, and he gladly agreed to her suggestions. He called for the cocktail cart and mixed their drinks in bed. They sipped and chatted.

"What's the book?" Missy asked, nodding toward a book lying on his nightstand.

"Something the Missus insists I have to read. She read it and was all taken with it. It's by Steinbeck and is called *The Grapes of Wrath.*"

Missy ran their movie on the sixteen-millimeter Bell & Howell projector that had been a gift to the President from the film industry. So he could see some of their latest films, they also supplied sixteen-millimeter prints. Tonight they saw *Stagecoach.*

The evening was warm. Missy put aside her peignoir. Her nightgown was not immodestly sheer. The President had plumped pillows for her, and she sat beside him on the bed.

"You're an angel to have stayed in Washington this weekend," he said. "It would have been damned lonely around here."

In the First Lady's bedroom, Mrs. Roosevelt sat at a card table in her nightgown. Lorena Hickock, just now shuffling the cards, wore pink silk pajamas. Hick no longer lived in the White House, as she had in some years past, but she visited often and was staying this weekend.

"Franklin thinks Stalin may be negotiating a non-aggression pact with Hitler," said Mrs. Roosevelt.

"Do you think so?" Hick asked.

"It seems difficult to believe."

"My darling, it is impossible to believe. Im . . . possible."

Mrs. Roosevelt woke to the jangling of the telephone beside her bed. She lifted the receiver.

"Yes?"

"Ma'am, this is Dominic Deconcini. We've arrested an intruder. It may possibly have something to do with the Lucinda Robinson murder. I thought you'd want to know."

"You've arrested whom? And where?"

"In the map room. And the person we've arrested is Mary Logan, one of the young people working in the Wilson archives."

"Mary Logan!"

"Yes, Ma'am. She was photographing the maps."

At the time of the Munich crisis the President had established a situation room on the ground floor of the White House, in the large room immediately to the west of the oval diplomatic reception room. Officers from army and navy intelligence worked in this room, not full-time but from time to time, formulating military and naval situation reports. To understand the developing Munich crisis, the President had wanted to know, as nearly as he could find out, what armed strength the several nations had at various places. Information was culled from a wide variety of sources: from the military and naval attachés at United States embassies, from trustworthy returning tourists, from refugees, from such information as the British and French intelligence services were willing to share, from newspapers, from Winston Churchill, who had his own sources superior in some respects to the official intelligence agencies' sources, and from a few spies.

The President was especially interested in knowing where naval power was stationed. He was interested, for example, in how construction was progressing on four great German battleships: *Scharnhorst*, *Gneisenau*, *Tirpitz*, and *Bismarck*. Among the documents in the situation room—more often called map room—were files, including photographs, of the four ships, all still unfinished.

On his own, without agreement from Admiral King or any others, the President had concluded that if the three German pocket battleships, *Deutschland*, *Admiral Scheer*, and *Admiral Graf Spee*, left their harbors and entered the Atlantic, war was imminent. The three were commerce raiders. Once war was declared, the British Home Fleet would bottle these ships up in the Baltic, blocking them at the Skagerrak or at worst in the North Sea. Therefore, they would sail a week or more before a war began. It would be a sure signal that war was about to happen, and the President insisted on knowing the whereabouts of the pocket battleships.

Much of the information the President wanted was in files stored in the situation room. Much more was marked on the huge maps that lined the walls.

Hardly anyone knew of the existence of the situation room. It was the kind of thing a wartime leader maintained. Some members of Congress would have considered it an act of aggression for the President of the United States even to have such a facility. Needless to say, it was kept carefully locked. The White House physician, who occupied the next room, did not know what was in that locked room. Neither did the housekeeper, Mrs. Nesbitt, whose office was two doors away.

"Where do you have the young woman now?" Mrs. Roosevelt asked Deconcini.

"For the moment we're holding Miss Logan in the doctor's office," said Deconcini.

"I shall be right down."

Hick had wakened. She had fallen asleep more than an hour earlier, lying on the bed and listening to a radio concert, and Mrs. Roosevelt had simply covered her with the sheet, which was the only bed covering she was using on this warm evening, and had barely wakened her. She touched Hick's hand and whispered she should go back to sleep. "I have to run a little errand."

"To the pee-pee?" asked Hick, yawning and still more than half asleep.

Mrs. Roosevelt nodded. "Yes. I'll be back shortly."

As Mrs. Roosevelt was dressing, Hick woke again. "Eleanor," she asked, "do they *usually* call you on the phone and tell you to go potty?"

The office of the White House physician was spartanly furnished. It contained a small yellow-oak desk, a matching swivel chair, and a glass-front case of books. It was not an examining room—the doctor had another room for that— but strictly an office. It contained also two yellow-oak armchairs.

The door to the office was now guarded by two uniformed White House policemen. Inside, Dominic Deconcini rested his backside against the desk and confronted Mary Logan, who sat in one of the armchairs.

The two looked as though they might have been brother and sister, Mrs. Roosevelt reflected as she stepped into the doorway and stared at them. Both had dark hair and sharp features. Both had olive complexions. Both apparently had a practiced skill for concealing their emotions behind bland faces. Mary Logan was under arrest, but she didn't seem troubled by it. She faced Deconcini, erect and apparently self-confident, and they appeared to have been carrying on a quiet conversation.

"I hope," said Mrs. Roosevelt, "I am going to learn that some kind of mistake has been made, or that there is some explanation for what seems to be the case."

"There is no mistake," said Deconcini. "She was— Well, let me show you what she was doing."

He picked up from the desk and handed to the First Lady a tiny stainless-steel object that looked a little like a box for two cigarettes or for a few wooden matches. She examined it and saw that it was a camera—a camera no more than three inches long, less than an inch wide, and no more than half an inch thick. Tiny as it was, the camera had focus control, exposure control, and a see-through viewfinder. Engraved in the stainless steel was an odd word: MINOX.

"She was photographing the maps," said Deconcini.

Mrs. Roosevelt glanced around the rooms at the maps. Markers showed the location of units of the army and marine corps within the United States. Maps of Europe showed where the American intelligence system thought German and French and Russian army divisions were. Maps of the Atlantic and Pacific showed the location of United States warships and the supposed location of principal British, French, German, and Japanese ships. Probably as important as the information charted on the maps was the simple fact that the United States was keeping track of all these things and had so much knowledge.

"Do you have an explanation for this, Miss Logan?" Mrs. Roosevelt asked.

"Yes. It's perfectly simple. *He* was taking pictures. I caught him at it."

Deconcini smiled ironically at Mrs. Roosevelt and shrugged.

Mrs. Roosevelt stared thoughtfully for a moment at Mary Logan, then turned to Deconcini and said, "I think you and I had better talk outside."

As they left the room, Deconcini slapped the leather handcuff case on the belt of one of the uniformed officers and said, "Make sure she doesn't try to leave."

"Or in fact to hurt herself," said Mrs. Roosevelt.

In the central hall outside, Deconcini explained that a White House policeman—the one inside with Mary Logan now in fact—had noticed light shining faintly under the door of the map room. He had summoned the other man, and together they had entered the room and seen the young woman photographing one of the maps. They had called the Secret Service office, and Deconcini had been the man on night duty.

"Who, besides the two officers and you and me, knows about this?" asked Mrs. Roosevelt.

"No one."

She sighed. "Technically, I suppose we should call the FBI. Espionage is—"

"I supposed the thing to do was call them after the case is completely solved and there is nothing more to be done," said Deconcini. "That way we won't have Hoover and his boys snooping around the White House."

"You haven't phoned Mr. Baines?"

"Not yet."

"Let him enjoy his day off. What could he do that you cannot? But I think we should telephone Captain Kennelly. Mary is going to have to be held in jail."

They returned to the doctor's office, where Mary Logan now sat with her left wrist handcuffed to her chair. Mrs. Roosevelt had the White House operator place the call to Kennelly, to tell him what was going on and ask if he would come.

"I am compelled to assume that you are in the employ of a foreign government," said Mrs. Roosevelt. "Do you realize that what you have done subjects you to a long term of imprisonment?"

Mary Logan looked up into the face of the First Lady and said nothing.

"The answer to one question is going to tell us a great deal about who she is and who she works for," said Deconcini. "How did you get into the White House after midnight?"

Mary Logan shrugged.

Mrs. Roosevelt picked up a small leather purse. "Is this hers?" she asked.

"Yes, Ma'am," said the White House policeman. "We haven't looked inside it yet. We were waiting for you."

Mrs. Roosevelt opened the little purse. The first thing she saw was a Baby Browning automatic, a vicious little 6.35mm pistol designed for one purpose: to fire shots into another person at point-blank range.

"Damn!" snorted the officer. "Lucky we caught her standing a few feet away from that."

Mrs. Roosevelt put the pistol aside and poured the rest of the contents of the purse on the desk. Besides the handkerchief, there was a bottle of pills, a room key, probably to her room at the boardinghouse where she had lived adjacent to Lucinda, a lipstick, a compact, and another key.

"No point in asking her what this key opens," said Mrs. Roosevelt. "Apparently she will not answer any questions."

Deconcini stared at the key. It was not a common latchkey but was a far more complex key, intended for a complex lock. The blade had a warding to guide it through an irregularly shaped keyway, and its serrations were designed to move five or six tumblers.

"I am going to make a guess as to what door that key opens," said Mrs. Roosevelt. "Come, Mr. Deconcini. Let's see if my guess is right."

She led Deconcini through the east hall. A sleepy policeman on duty at the east door of the ground floor opened the door for them, and they walked through the arcade, where another policeman guarded the door to the East Wing. He let them in and asked if he should accompany them. Mrs. Roosevelt told him no, she knew where she was going.

In the East Wing she led Deconcini down the steps into the bomb shelter built in 1934. A locked steel door blocked access to the tunnel to the cellar of the Treasury Building.

"Now we shall see what this key is for," she said.

She inserted the key in the lock and turned it with success. She turned the knob and pushed on the door. It swung back. The tunnel under East Executive Avenue lay open before them.

"It's also a confidential escape from the White House," she told Deconcini. "Distinguished visitors who didn't want to face reporters have occasionally left the White House this way. Although this president couldn't use it, I suppose another idea was to provide an escape route in the event the White House were ever assaulted by a mob."

The lights were on in the tunnel. Deconcini followed Mrs. Roosevelt as she walked through. At the end they faced a flight of concrete steps. At the top was another locked door. The same key opened that door, and in a moment they were in the cellar of the old Treasury Building.

No guard interrupted their progress as they climbed to the

main floor and walked to a door that opened off the west facade of the Treasury Building. From inside, it could be opened without a key, and they left the building and stood on East Executive Avenue.

"The key is good for opening one more door somewhere," said Mrs. Roosevelt. "I'm afraid I don't know which. We could try several, but I suspect our best course is to return to the White House through the North Portico.

The night was warm. A breeze that carried a fresh, fragrant odor of rain up from Virginia made the night pleasant. The orange glow of the late-night city reddened clouds that hung low and promised a refreshing shower. The red light atop the Washington Monument winked reassuringly. (Why it should have been reassuring was uncertain. It had not blinked when Mrs. Roosevelt first lived in Washington, during the Wilson presidency. It had been blinking when she came back in 1933 and had blinked unceasingly ever since. Airplane pilots appreciated it, and so did she.) The after-midnight city was not quiet. An uneven low roar laid over it, composed of sounds that didn't carry so well in the day: the distant rumbling of railway trains, the higher-pitched roar of muffled truck and automobile engines, a hum that was perhaps from big fans in ventilating systems, all punctuated irregularly with blasts of locomotive whistles, the honk of horns, and even laughs and shouts of summer-night revelers still on the streets.

It occurred to Mrs. Roosevelt that she had never before been on the streets of Washington after midnight. She had often been driven through those streets after midnight, on her way home from some affair or other, but she had never before been a pedestrian on these after-midnight streets. She wondered if her attitude toward the city might be different if she had.

She and Deconcini reentered the White House through the northeast gate, astonishing the policeman on duty there.

They astonished also the desk sergeant in the north portico. Shortly they were back on the ground floor, where they found that Ed Kennelly had just arrived.

"We have learned something," she told Kennelly. "The key carried in Miss Logan's purse is the key to the doors to the Treasury tunnel. That explains how she got into the house after midnight."

"It could explain how someone got into the house after midnight to move the body of Lucinda Robinson," said Kennelly.

"My own thought as well," said the First Lady.

"One problem solved maybe."

"Which only deepens the mystery," said Mrs. Roosevelt. "Where did she get the key?"

"Plus, who is she, and why did she have a key, and what the devil was she doing?" Deconcini added.

"She refuses to answer any question whatever," said Mrs. Roosevelt.

"We can cure that in short order," said Kennelly.

"And with just what technique would you 'cure' it?" asked the First Lady.

"Strip her down, 'cuff her to a chair in a room in the basement, and squirt her with a fire hose. She'll talk."

Mrs. Roosevelt shook her head. "You know I don't like such techniques, even when applied to a man," she said.

"I bet she'd talk before I ever turned on the water," said Kennelly.

She smiled at him: warmly yet with reserve. "You and I have philosophical differences," she said.

"I'm just a rough, rude cop . . . Ma'am."

She shook her head fervently. "No. But we have different ways of approaching things . . . Captain Kennelly."

She read Kennelly's smile. No one else did.

"Well, I see no choice but to take the pretty colleen here

and lock her up. She may decide she wants to tell us a few things after she's spent the night in the lockup."

Mrs. Roosevelt returned to the doctor's office. "Miss Logan," she said quietly. "Unless you want to answer some questions, you will have to be removed to jail now."

Mary Logan sneered. "And will I be let loose if I do answer?" she asked. "I don't think so. You're going to put me in jail either way. I'm not stupid, Mrs. Roosevelt."

The First Lady shook her head. "I'm afraid you may well be, dear," she said.

Hick was awake, sitting up, listening to an all-night radio station and reading *The Grapes of Wrath* when Mrs. Roosevelt returned to her bedroom. A pot of coffee and a plate of cookies sat on a table.

"How thoughtful!"

"Has the world fallen apart?" Hick asked.

"A spy was caught in the White House," said Mrs. Roosevelt. She began to undress. "A young woman of my acquaintance was caught tonight, photographing confidential documents."

"Confidential . . . About what?"

"My darling Hick," said the First Lady, "you must understand that in the past two or three years the world has become a far more dangerous place. Time was, there were no secrets, except things like plans for the next campaign, the details of a bill before it was introduced in Congress . . . things like that. Today— Can you keep secrets?"

"Absolutely."

"The isolationists, in the Congress and out, would shriek and howl if they knew the President tries to keep track of the strength and whereabouts of foreign military and naval units. Hick . . . he has a war room, just as he would have to do if the nation were at war, and tonight a young woman penetrated that room and was caught photographing the confidential documents and maps kept there."

"God, the world is closing in on us!" said Hick. She poured coffee as Mrs. Roosevelt slipped out of the rest of her clothes and pulled on a nightgown. "It seemed ridiculous to me when Neville Chamberlain spoke of Czechoslovakia as 'a faraway people of whom we know little.' At the time, a year ago, I thought it was *we* to whom Czechoslovakia was far away. Now it doesn't seem so far away at all. What you've just told me makes Europe seem very close indeed."

"A very deep secret, Hick."

"Understood. I'll subdue my lifelong journalistic instincts. It has to be, doesn't it, that this spy was working for the German government?"

"I can't think of anyone else for whom she could have been working," said Mrs. Roosevelt.

"A German?"

"I would guess not," said Mrs. Roosevelt. "I would think an American, corrupted into working for the Nazis. Although her demeanor suggested she was long trained for what she was doing. I should have thought she would have been frightened. If she was, she concealed it resolutely."

"And now she's in jail."

"Yes, or on her way there, in any event."

"God, what kind of world do we live in!"

Ed Kennelly dozed at his desk. He had turned Mary Logan over to the jail matrons, instructing them to search her thoroughly and report to him when they were finished.

"Captain . . ."

"Uh . . . yeah?"

The senior police matron on duty that night had taken responsibility for Mary Logan. Her name was Donna Monroe: a beefy blonde woman with a flushed face, who wore round gold-rimmed spectacles. "We lost her, Captain," she said grimly.

"Huh? *Whatta ya mean ya lost her?*"

"She's dead, Captain! She killed herself."

Kennelly saw that the woman was shaken, and he pointed to a chair. "In simple words, Monroe," he said dully.

"We took her back. We stripped her. We put her in the shower and turned on the water. I turned around to get a towel off the shelf, and when I turned again and looked at her, she was on the floor of the shower, rolling around and choking. I shut off the water and got down over her. I forced her mouth open and ran my finger down her throat, thinking she was choking on something. That wasn't it. She gagged, but she didn't upchuck anything.

"Brown, who was working with me, was already on the phone, screaming for a doctor. By the time the doc got there, the prisoner was dead."

Kennelly picked up his telephone and dialed the White House. He pulled a bottle of bourbon from a desk drawer, took a swig, and handed the bottle to the matron.

Mrs. Roosevelt stepped aside, into a recess in the hallway, and Kennelly stopped with her. Lorena Hickock, who had come from the White House with her, was a few paces ahead with Matron Donna Monroe.

"Ed . . ."

The First Lady wiped tears from her cheeks. He took her hand and kissed it.

"I brought Hick with me because I didn't know if I could face this alone."

"You don't have to see her."

Mrs. Roosevelt drew a deep breath. "I haven't backed away from things before," she said.

"No, you haven't."

"Well, I won't back away from this, either. But I must tell you . . . two corpses laid out in the morgue within one week—" She shook her head but recovered her composure. "Let's see her," she said resolutely.

Lorena Hickock held her hand tightly over her mouth, as if to hold back vomit. The body of Mary Logan lay as Lucinda Robinson's had: naked, on its back, ghastly pale and still, with the eyes open.

"Cyanide poisoning, self-administered," said the young doctor who stood at the head of the table. "My name is Dr. Paul Dryer, Ma'am."

Mrs. Roosevelt smelled a strange sweet odor in the room. She had heard and now remembered that cyanide had an odor like sugared almonds. "How in the world?"

"I found tiny shards of glass in her mouth and throat, Ma'am. She'd had the capsule in her mouth and bit down on it."

"She carried it in what we supposed was a lipstick," said Kennelly. He had examined all of Mary Logan's property again while Mrs. Roosevelt was on her way to headquarters. "Inside the lipstick case there was a little brass cylinder with a screw cap. The capsule had been in the cylinder, beyond doubt. When she put it in her mouth, we can't tell. Maybe she was carrying it all the time she was in the White House."

"She understood probably that when she came out of the shower we would do a body-cavity search," said Donna Monroe. "That's standard procedure in a case as serious as this was."

Mrs. Roosevelt's lip trembled as she stared at the corpse. "She didn't say a word, didn't answer a question . . . What kind of person was she? Where did she come from?"

"Carrying that tiny camera . . ." said Kennelly, "also the pistol and the poison, I guess it's pretty clear what kind of person she was and where she came from."

"It is very difficult for me to understand," said Mrs. Roosevelt sadly.

"We were talking about what kind of world we live in," said Lorena Hickock.

"There is something more, Ma'am," said Dr. Dryer. "He pointed to a small stainless-steel cylinder lying on a wheeled table beside the examining table. I found that— I found that, Ma'am, in a very private part of the body. She was carrying a fortune in gems."

The jewels were lying on the table beside the cylinder. Twenty or more of them, glittering diamonds mostly, with also two or three green stones that had to be emeralds.

Hick gaped. "She had that in—?" She pointed.

Dr. Dryer nodded.

Mrs. Roosevelt frowned at the matron and asked, "Would *you* have found that?"

"Yes, Ma'am."

"You'd have searched—?"

The matron nodded. "Not ordinary drunks and shoplifters. But serious cases. It's not awfully unusual to find something, though I never saw a cylinder like that before."

"What do you find?"

"Money, mostly. Rolled fifty-dollar or hundred-dollar bills, wrapped in cellophane and Scotch tape. If we don't find it when they come in, they pull it out at night and hide it in their cots. They tuck it back in in the morning."

Mrs. Roosevelt glanced at Hick. "I grew up in a more innocent time."

"No, Ma'am," said the matron. "It's nothing new."

"Men do the same thing," said Kennelly. "Except—" He tossed his head back over his shoulder.

"I wish I hadn't heard all this," said the First Lady. She sighed. "This changes everything. It's not of course certain that this relates in any way to the death of Lucinda Robinson."

"I'm going to bet it does," said Kennelly.

Lorena Hickock, who had hung back during most of her time in this room, had now moved closer and was staring hard at the body. "Say," she said. "This girl was a blonde. She dyed her hair."

IX

Mrs. Roosevelt telephoned the President early on Sunday morning, at an hour when she judged she would not be wakening him but when he had not yet ordered his breakfast tray. She asked him to join her for breakfast in the private dining room at nine o'clock. She told him Lorena Hickock had spent the night in the White House and that she would like to have her join them, since Hick knew all about what they had to discuss. The President agreed to that, and when he appeared in the dining room Missy was with him.

"Something extremely distressing happened last night," Mrs. Roosevelt said to the President. "A spy was caught in your situation room. She was photographing the maps when she was caught. Her film has been developed, and I am told this morning that she had also photographed quite a few documents from the files."

"*She?* Who is she? How did she get into the White House?" the President asked.

"Her name was Mary Logan," said Mrs. Roosevelt. "She was one of the young people hired to work on the Wilson archives."

"Do I understand you to say her name *was* Mary Logan?" asked Missy. "She—?"

"She is dead," said Mrs. Roosevelt. "She was carrying a poison capsule in her mouth and crushed it just before she would have been subjected to what is called a body-cavity search."

"A 'body cavity search'?" asked the President. "What in the world is a body-cavity search?"

"Your imagination may suggest what it is," said Mrs. Roosevelt. "In another . . . cavity she was carrying a fortune in gems. The young woman was obviously a well-trained, fully committed spy."

"How did she get into the White House?"

"Through the Treasury tunnel. So the question is, how did she obtain a key?"

The President shook his head. He put down his coffee cup without taking his intended sip. "This is very, very serious, Babs," he said. "We will have to call in the FBI. As much as I dislike having J. Edgar Hoover and his boys prowling around the White House, we cannot exclude the FBI from this investigation. Espionage is an FBI responsibility. If it came to the attention of the press that we had failed to report a case like this to the Bureau, the scandal would take on gigantic proportions."

"If we could solve the problem quickly," said Mrs. Roosevelt, "we could present Director Hoover with a fait accompli and not have to endure him snooping around the White House."

"Babs, I have made jokes about your meddling in the investigation of crimes. I think you understand, though, that I admire the help you have given to the Secret Service and the police. I am grateful for it, too. But this is a job for the pros, and I don't see how we can exclude the FBI. I am going to have to call Edgar Hoover."

"Couldn't we call Mr. Martin Willoughby?" asked Mrs. Roosevelt.

The President fixed his eye on Lorena Hickock. "Hick," he said, "this conversation is covering some very deep, dark secrets."

"I'll leave if you want," said Hick.

"No. I just want you to understand they *are* important secrets. Now, Babs, no, we can't use Brother Willoughby. We've got an informant inside the FBI, and we mustn't compromise him the first time we need a service. He's too important to us."

"So we must have Mr. Hoover, then. Yes, I suppose we must."

The President caused a degree of consternation in the White House when he descended on the west elevator and wheeled himself toward the Oval Office early in the afternoon. The few people in the West Wing on Sunday afternoon had not expected him and were embarrassed to be seen without their jackets or neckties—two secretaries, indeed, without their shoes.

He wheeled himself with his customary strong strokes, through the colonnade, past the swimming pool and rose garden, and into the west wing. Pausing in the hall, he looked into the lobby and saw J. Edgar Hoover waiting.

"Brother Hoover! C'mon! Sorry to have called you in on Sunday afternoon, but I think we can make this short."

Mrs. Roosevelt was waiting in the Oval Office, as was Ed Kennelly.

"You know Captain Kennelly of the D.C. police, I imagine," said the President.

"Yes, we've met," said Hoover, and he extended a hand to be shaken.

"Pleasure, Director," said Kennelly.

The President sat behind his desk, lifting himself out of his wheelchair and planting himself in his upholstered armchair. With his arms he lifted his legs onto the box under his desk, putting them in a more comfortable position. He had come down from the second floor in an odd suit of clothes: a worn linen jacket, once white but now yellowed, a white shirt with a black bow tie, and wrinkled white trousers. All of this was in distinct contrast to the crisp light-blue double-breasted suit worn by Hoover, who also carried a Panama hat and had put it aside on a table.

"An odd event befell the White House last night, Edgar," said the President. "Ed can probably tell it most succinctly."

Kennelly used as few words as possible in telling Hoover of the arrest and death of Mary Logan. Mrs. Roosevelt added only that she and Agent Deconcini had used the key found in Miss Logan's purse to open the doors in the Treasury tunnel.

"I assume you knew, Edgar, that we have a situation room in the White House," said the President.

"As a matter of fact, I did not, Mr. President. It's a matter for the War and Navy Departments and not within my jurisdiction."

"It's of course a national secret," said the President.

"I will treat anything I learn in the White House as a national secret," said Hoover ingenuously.

"Good. Please do," said the President. "The point is, that when a spy is found photographing documents, it becomes a matter for your jurisdiction. All this was discovered in the middle of the night. I called you as soon as it was brought to my attention. In the meanwhile, I think Captain Kennelly and Mr. Deconcini of the Secret Service, with some . . . interference by my wife, have done a good job of getting at the basic facts."

Hoover nodded at Mrs. Roosevelt and Ed Kennelly. "I am grateful," he said.

"We've got no local record of her fingerprints," said Kennelly. "I'm hoping you do."

"Is it your supposition that she was a German?" asked Hoover. "Is it not equally possible that she worked for the Communist conspiracy?"

"Equally possible, Brother Hoover," said the President. "That's what we want you to find out."

"I'd like to submit a copy of her fingerprints to MI5, British Intelligence," said Hoover. "Of course, you can't do that on Sunday. The British are still firm believers in their weekends. But tomorrow . . ."

"You will have them," said Kennelly.

"You've made photographs of her?"

"Yes, and we've searched her room in the boardinghouse where she lived."

"You should understand, Director Hoover," said Mrs. Roosevelt, "that Mary Logan was a close friend of Lucinda Robinson. Until now we had not supposed there could be any espionage connection involved in the murder of Lucinda Robinson. Now, we have to wonder."

"The bodies?" asked Hoover.

"Lucinda has been taken home to Minnesota by her parents, and buried," said Mrs. Roosevelt. She looked to Kennelly.

"I think we'll keep Mary in cold storage for a while."

"She said she was from Baltimore," said Mrs. Roosevelt. "If a family claims her—"

"*If,*" said Kennelly. "I'll be surprised if she was from Baltimore or if anything else in her personnel file is true."

"There is no one in the NYA office on Sunday," said Mrs. Roosevelt. "Her file can be checked tomorrow."

When Hoover had left, Mrs. Roosevelt and Ed Kennelly hung back in the Oval Office for a moment, instinctively perhaps, maybe defensively.

"It would be good," said the President, "if this matter could be settled *toute de suite.*"

"I got one more piece of information," said Kennelly. "We can give it to the Director when we want to, *if* we want to. We went over that little camera for fingerprints. I mean, we went over every smidgen of it. And on the little film cartridge— Say, those tiny little cartridges hold enough film to make *fifty* pictures. Can you imagine? Anyway, the camera had one set of prints on it, plus some unreadable smudges. But the film cartridge had another set on it."

" 'The Kraut!' " Mrs. Roosevelt exclaimed.

"I wish," said Kennelly. "But no. Almost as interesting. The prints on the cartridge are Lucinda Robinson's."

"Another thing almost as interesting," said Kennelly as he and Mrs. Roosevelt walked through the colonnade on their way back to the White House proper. "That roll of film was good for fifty shots. My photo lab man was very careful with it. He cut pieces off, a couple of inches at a time, and experimented with different ways of developing it—different chemicals and times—until he got the best combination for the clearest pictures. He says the camera and film are a scientific miracle, incidentally. Anyway, the first four shots taken seem to have been somebody experimenting with the camera, learning how to use it. They are pictures of a room. What room? No way to tell."

"If we could find the room—"

"Yeah, sure. If we could. Then there are two more shots. Whoever was experimenting turned the camera down and took pictures of her own feet."

"And of course we can't tell whose feet," said Mrs. Roosevelt.

"Right. We can't tell. But, uh . . . Whoever she was, she was stark naked. She'd focused on her feet, and they're sharp in the pictures; but you can see enough in the blurry part to see she was female—not enough to tell if she was Lucinda or Mary."

Mrs. Roosevelt shook her head. "That doesn't tell us very much, does it? In fact, it could have been someone else entirely."

"Except that the fingerprints prove that Mary handled the camera and Lucinda handled the film cartridge. I'd call it likely that Lucinda handled the camera, but her fingerprints were smudged over by Mary's."

"Reasonable," said Mrs. Roosevelt.

"One thing more. Also in good focus, on the floor, is a man's foot. Very close to the girl's. Foot . . . I should say a shoe. And a trouser leg. He was dressed. He was teaching her to use the camera. Or so I'd guess."

"I'll guess something more," said Mrs. Roosevelt. "It was Lucinda. From what we know of Mary, I'd judge she already knew how to use the camera."

"I didn't want to invite Director Hoover into the Robinson investigation," said Kennelly. "We'd have to tell him *every-thing.*"

"Maybe we should have told the President, however," said Mrs. Roosevelt.

The President spoke to Baines that afternoon. Although Mrs. Roosevelt had been reluctant to call the senior agent in on Sunday, the President—maybe not knowing what long hours the man had kept during the past week—asked him to come to the presidential study on the second floor.

Jerry Baines found the President in his shirtsleeves, working again on his stamp collection.

"You know what happened?" the President asked.

"Dom Deconcini told me," said Baines.

"Where did that key come from?" asked the President. "Not many people even know about the Treasury tunnel.

Only very few have keys. If we're not to have John Edgar Hoover prying into everything in the establishment, we're going to have to find out how Miss Mary Logan came into possession of a key to the doors to the treasury tunnel. Do you have a list of people to whom keys have been issued?"

"Yes, Sir. It's a very short list, I promise you. Even you don't have one, Mr. President. Mrs. Roosevelt doesn't have one. I have one. The chief of the uniformed White House police has one. Miss LeHand has one. General Watson has one. Mr. Howe had one before he died, but when he went to the hospital he returned it. Mr. Hopkins has one."

"Is that all?"

"Yes, Sir. Others have been allowed to use keys from time to time, but they have to be signed out and signed back in within a specified time."

"During that time, could someone have had a copy ground?"

"No, Sir. The key is too complex. Besides, the key bears a code telling any locksmith who is asked to make a duplicate to check first with the police. I can't say it's impossible to copy the key, but it would be very difficult."

"Priority one, Brother Baines," said the President. "We've got to know. In any case, fasten the doors some other way overnight, and tomorrow change the locks. The same with the situation room. Apparently the young woman picked that lock—meaning that she was an accomplished yegg but meaning also the lock is not good enough."

That Sunday evening the Marine Band played a concert on the south lawn. The President was wheeled out on the South Portico, where he could see the crowd and the crowd could see him. E Street was closed, and the crowd overflowed the lawn and stood in the street and on the Ellipse.

Mrs. Roosevelt stood beside the President for a while, then

went down and walked out among the people. Two Secret Service agents stayed near her—not Baines or Deconcini. The crowd was happy, in an easy mood. The evening was warm, and the people appreciated the opportunity to be out of doors and to be entertained by the concert. They recognized the tall woman in the simple, flowing white summer dress, and they called friendly greetings to the First Lady. She responded by smiling, nodding, and waving.

The band played spirited marches—"On the Mall," "Stars and Stripes Forever"—together with popular songs such as "Who's Afraid of the Big Bad Wolf?" and "Hi-Ho, Hi-Ho, It's Off to Work We Go." The concert ended with the playing of "The Star Spangled Banner," during which fireworks were shot into the air from a barge in the Tidal Basin.

After the concert, Mrs. Roosevelt went to the Morgenthaus for dinner. Lorena Hickock and Joseph Lash had been invited, too. The President and Missy retired to his bedroom for dinner trays from the White House kitchen and an evening of music from records and the radio.

Monday morning J. Edgar Hoover arrived at the White House at nine, accompanied by Martin Willoughby.

"Why you, Willoughby?" Baines asked when he could take the agent aside for a moment. "Has he figured it out?"

Willoughby shook his head. "The White House was my assignment, so it's my assignment again."

"Well," said Hoover enthusiastically. "Does the President want to see us?"

"I don't think so," said Baines. "I believe Mrs. Roosevelt would like to see you."

Hoover and Willoughby sat down with the First Lady a few minutes later, in her office. Baines was not with them. He was off in pursuit of what the President had called the first priority.

"Well, Ma'am," said Hoover with obvious satisfaction, "I have some interesting information."

"I am very glad to hear it, Mr. Director," she said. "I was confident you would come up with something important very quickly."

Hoover's face clouded. He could not be sure if she meant what she said or were poking gentle fun at him. He drew a deep breath. "MI5 in London has been most cooperative," he said. "Do you realize we can now send fingerprints to London and Paris the same way the news wires can send and receive photographs?"

"We live in a technological age," said Mrs. Roosevelt.

"We transmitted the prints to London very early this morning—not so early London time. MI5 carried them immediately to Scotland Yard, Special Branch. Special Branch—Well, here is the return transmission." He handed her a piece of paper. "Interesting, isn't it."

She read—

> The fingerprints you have transmitted are those of Ana Becker, a German national. The following is our summary of her record.
>
> Becker, Ana, aka Frieda Hirsch, Betty Brown, and Deborah Flynn. Born 1906. Arrested Munich, 1925 for pouring kerosene into a ballot box and igniting it. Identified as ardent member of National Socialist German Workers Party (NAZIs). Arrested various times by Bavarian, Berlin authorities for rioting and inciting to riot. No further German criminal record after 1929. Believed to be an intimate of one Otto Ohlendorf, a high-ranking officer of the SS and SD (*Sicherheitsdienst*, the security service of the Nazi Party).
>
> Ana Becker was arrested in London in 1934, on a charge of espionage brought by Special Branch. Re-

leased to the German Embassy and allowed to leave
the country. On this occasion she used the alias
Betty Brown. She was arrested and deported by
Irish authorities in 1935, then using the alias Debo-
rah Flynn.

Ana Becker is believed to be a trained and dedi-
cated German agent, working not within conven-
tional German military intelligence but within the
independent espionage services of the Nazi Party,
the SS, and the SD. She speaks fluent English and is
clever in adapting it to various accents.

"It's distressing, isn't it," Hoover asked, "to think that this
woman was working within the White House under the auspices of the National Youth Administration?"

"Distressing indeed," said Mrs. Roosevelt.

"We can't be too careful," said Hoover.

"Oh, I believe we can, Director Hoover. If we abolished
programs like the N.Y.A. for fear that subversives might
somehow penetrate them occasionally and use them for il-
licit purposes, then we would lose the benefits of programs
that have done a very great deal of good for very many people."

"Well, I didn't mean to suggest we abolish—"

"I realize you didn't," she said with a smile. "And this information you have obtained is very helpful. I am beginning to
understand some things that were deeply mysterious
before."

Jerry Baines sat across a desk from Harry Hopkins.

"Key . . ." muttered Hopkins with a frown. "Key, of course.
Where the hell is the damned thing?"

"Where did you keep it, Mr. Hopkins?"

"Right here in my desk drawer. Center drawer. But—"

"It's missing," said Baines.

Hopkins sighed and nodded. "It's missing. Damned if it isn't."

"Let's assume you didn't just lose it," said Baines. "If you didn't just mislay it, then who might have taken it? Who, besides yourself, has access to the drawers of your desk? Put in another way, who has access to your office when you are not in it?"

Knowing that Director Hoover had gone to the archives office and suspecting he might have questioned the young people there rather sharply, Mrs. Roosevelt went there just before noon. She spoke to the little group. Cynthia Phillips and Betty Fulk were crying. Christian Cassell appeared to be in a state of shock.

"I am sorry that the tragic news about Mary Logan came to you from Director Hoover. I should have preferred to bring it to you myself, but it is an FBI investigation, and I did not want to seem to be meddling. I assume Director Hoover emphasized to you the extremely confidential nature of the matter."

"What Mr. Hoover told us is absolutely unbelievable," said Cassell.

"Yes. I should be grateful, Mr. Cassell, if you would come to my office with me. I'd like to go over one or two more things with you."

He walked through the ground floor corridor with the First Lady, and they used the stairs rather than an elevator to go to the second floor.

"Mr. Cassell," she said when they were seated in her office, "you were intimately acquainted with Lucinda Robinson, as you have acknowledged. Is it possible you were a good friend of Mary Logan, too? I'm not suggesting an intimate friend. Did you have dates with Mary Logan?"

"No, Ma'am. I never saw her outside the office."

"She gave a Baltimore address. The Baltimore police have responded to an inquiry this morning, saying she did indeed have a home there. But it is a room in a boardinghouse, on which she was paying the rent. It is not her family home."

"We always understood that the job in the Wilson archives is temporary. Maybe she wanted to keep a room she liked and expected to go back to."

"Perhaps . . . But an N.Y.A. job does not pay generously. Could she afford to keep two rooms for ten months?"

"I have no idea. Apparently she could."

"Obviously there was a great deal more to her than we knew. Obviously she wasn't living on what she was paid by the N.Y.A."

"I wonder who she really was," said Cassell.

"We know who she really was," said Mrs. Roosevelt. "Her name was Ana Becker. She was a German national and a member of a Nazi spy organization."

"My Lord! How do you know?"

"From her fingerprints. They are on record in London, where she was arrested for espionage some years ago."

"Unbelievable!"

Tommy Thompson came in and whispered to Mrs. Roosevelt that Director Hoover would like to see her.

"It seems I must speak with Mr. Hoover. So, thank you, Mr. Cassell. Maybe we will talk again later."

J. Edgar Hoover sat down in the chair the First Lady indicated. "I notice you were talking to Cassell," he said. "I had agents check the home addresses given by each of the N.Y.A. people working in the archives. They are all valid. Even Mary Logan/Ana Becker had a room in a boardinghouse at the address shown in her personnel file. We were able to try the telephone number Cassell gave. An aunt answered. She confirmed that Chris, as she calls him, lives with her and her husband and is now in Washington on a temporary job. Since he speaks German, I thought possibly— Well, you know."

"I understand. A similar thought occurred to me."

"Lucinda Robinson also spoke German, did she not?" asked the Director. "Don't you think *her* death is somehow related to this matter?"

"I . . . suspect so. I can give you a brief account of what Mr. Baines and Captain Kennelly have so far learned about the murder of Lucinda Robinson."

Mrs. Roosevelt talked to him for fifteen minutes. She was most reluctant to do it, but she did not see what else she could do.

After a light lunch, Mrs. Roosevelt walked through the colonnade toward the West Wing. She meant to talk to Harry Hopkins about finding a way to get around the obstruction some Southern senators were offering to the use of federal funds to improve hospitals for Negroes. Just inside the West Wing she encountered Missy.

"Oh," said Missy. "I'm glad to see you. Wasn't that a horrible thing last night? You must not have had any sleep all night."

"I had a little," said Mrs. Roosevelt. "I was afraid I wouldn't be able to go back to sleep after seeing the body, but I suppose emotional exhaustion puts one to sleep very effectively."

"I'd like to ask you a question, if you don't mind."

"By all means," said the First Lady.

"A couple of hours ago I saw you walking up the stairs with a young man: handsome, light-haired, big fellow. If I'm not intruding, could you tell me who he is?"

"His name is Christian Cassell. He is one of the young people working on the Wilson archives project."

"I've seen him around the White House many times and never could identify him," said Missy. "He's very personable, always smiles and nods when we pass, but I never knew who he was."

"Where have you seen him, Missy?"

"Oh, uh . . . in the colonnade, here in the West Wing . . . around."

"Often?"

"I wouldn't say often. Occasionally."

"How very interesting," said Mrs. Roosevelt.

Next she met Jerry Baines coming through the central hall of the West Wing. They stopped to talk.

"Mr. Hopkins's key to the treasury tunnel is missing," Baines told her. "He kept it in the center drawer of his desk. He doesn't know how long it's been missing, since he almost never used it. The keys aren't numbered, so we don't know if the one the dead girl had is the one Mr. Hopkins had."

"The dead girl, Mr. Baines, turns out to have been ten years older than we thought. The FBI found a record of her, with British intelligence."

"The key's no good now, anyway," said Baines. "Workmen are changing the locks right now. The new keys will be numbered, and we'll know who has each one. It's locking the barn after the horse got out, but—"

"It's troubling to think of the new danger in the world," said the First Lady. "When Abraham Lincoln was President, any citizen could simply walk into the White House, go up to the anteroom of his office, and ask to see the President. Now . . ."

"My question is, who had access to Mr. Hopkins's desk?" said Baines.

"We know one person who could have," said Mrs. Roosevelt. "Mr. Lasky worked for Harry. I suppose he had access to his office. Perhaps we should question Mr. Lasky once more."

* * *

"That's going to be a little difficult," said Dominic Deconcini. "Lasky showed up for about ten minutes this morning, then disappeared again."

Carmine Plumeri, reached by telephone, swore he had not seen David Lasky. "The kid's crazy to have ducked out again. Tell ya what I'll do. I'll call his old man in Florida. Dave's not gonna run far without checking in with his father. I'll have him tell Dave he's making a hell of a mess for himself."

"I appreciate it," said Kennelly. "You tell him we took it easy on the young man, but we can't take it easy again. Unless he really did murder Lucinda Robinson, he's only making trouble for himself. Either way, we're gonna catch up with him sooner or later. He's not the kinda kid that can disappear permanent."

"Right, for sure," said Plumeri. "I'll give his old man the word."

Fred Mariott was determined to stick with it, to earn promotion, to make a career as a District police detective. Some of the jobs Captain Kennelly gave him challenged his determination.

For example, this Monday afternoon he was going from locksmith to locksmith, all over the District, looking for one who might have been asked to grind a key that carried a code saying it was not to be duplicated. The dreadful part of the job was, if he didn't find one, Kennelly might order him to start visiting hardware stores and dime stores.

As of four o'clock he had visited eleven locksmiths. Now he walked into the twelfth: Hindeman's Lock and Key, on M Street.

He identified himself. "Detective Sergeant Mariott, District PD. I want to ask about a key."

The man behind the counter, shrunken in old age, with dry skin and a mouth that turned down at the corners, shrugged and said, "I just grind keys, Sergeant. I don't ask what people want with 'em."

"Some keys can't be duplicated, right?" said Mariott.

"There ain't no key that can't be duplicated. Me, *I* can't duplicate any key, 'cause I ain't got the machinery. But there's no such key that the right man can't make another one just like it, open the same lock."

"Some keys have marks on, saying don't copy, call the cops. Right?"

"Yeah. Some keys say that. Nobody takes it seriously."

"Have you had a key in here in the last month or two that had that kind of mark?"

The old man nodded. "Two or three times. Too complicated. Couldn't copy 'em, no matter what it said on 'em."

"How 'bout a girl?" asked Mariott. "A girl hand you a key you couldn't copy?"

"Yeah. Some time back. Couldn't copy it. Took one look at it and told her I couldn't copy it."

"So what'd she do?"

"Walked out."

"You didn't call the police?"

"Nobody ever calls the police about one of those. If I coulda made it. If I could've copied it, I'd've called. But— What the hell? She walked out. I didn't know who she was."

Mariott pulled a photograph from a yellow envelope. "Is that the girl?" he asked.

The old man's eyes widened. "Hey, that's a stiff! That's a corpse!"

"That's the problem," said Mariott dryly.

"Yeah. That's the girl. She's the one. She was in here with a complicated key I couldn't begin to copy. Maybe a month ago. Maybe six weeks. I'm not sure."

* * *

That evening the President and Mrs. Roosevelt attended a cocktail reception and dinner given by the Polish ambassador.

The Polish Embassy was not on Embassy Row but a mile or so away on Meredith Hill. The Polish ambassador, Janosz Kuniczak, made a brave display, extending invitations to every embassy in Washington—even to that of the pitiful rump state that was all that remained of Czechoslovakia after, not just Germany but also Hungary and Poland, had taken bites out of it. It was a formal diplomatic occasion, and men arrived in uniforms and white tie, many wearing arrays of decorations. The embassy was lighted with thousands of candles. Guests might have gone swimming in the quantity of vintage champagne that was poured. They could glut themselves on caviar. A string orchestra played, mostly Chopin.

Mrs. Roosevelt had a sense of what was going on. Having eaten Czechoslovakia alive, Hitler had now turned his attention to two seaports: Memel, in Lithuania, and Danzig, supposedly a free port but actually handed over to Poland by the Treaty of Versailles. Both ports had been German before 1919. It had become obvious to everyone that Hitler intended to take the two cities if the Lithuanians and Poles would not give them up. The German ambassador was here this evening, received with studied courtesy. But so of course were the British and French, with whose nations Poland had a treaty of mutual defense.

That the President, who usually did not attend these functions, was wheeled into the grand rooms of the embassy was intended as an unsubtle message to Hitler.

Secretary of State and Mrs. Cordell Hull remained close to Mrs. Roosevelt for a time, but they drifted off. That did not leave her alone. She had been attending diplomatic receptions since 1933 and knew most of the people here.

The wife of the Swedish ambassador, Greta Bergstrom,

was a favorite of the American First Lady. Mrs. Bergstrom was tall, slender, blonde, and strikingly handsome. She spoke flawless, British-accented English.

"Mrs. Roosevelt. What a very great pleasure!"

"Mrs. Bergstrom. I had hoped to see you here."

The tall Swede glanced around the room. "I wonder when again so many of us will be gathered in one embassy. We will be neutral. You will be neutral. But, so many will be bitter enemies."

"I fear it," said Mrs. Roosevelt.

"So do I. We are closer. We will see the flashes of guns, hear the roar, and pray we may maintain our neutrality. For you to remain neutral will be much more difficult."

"President Wilson tried and failed," said Mrs. Roosevelt.

"Yes . . . Oh. I was sorry to read in the newspapers of the death of your assistant social secretary. She was a charming girl, wasn't she?"

"She was a dear girl," said Mrs. Roosevelt.

"I met her one time," said Mrs. Bergstrom. "She was a fine, dignified representative of America."

Mrs. Roosevelt smiled, yet frowned. "Where did you meet her, Mrs. Bergstrom?"

"At the German embassy," said Mrs. Bergstrom. "She was there, as a guest, escorted by a handsome young man. It was a small party. Most of the guests were Germans. We were invited . . . the Norwegians and Danes. I am embarrassed to admit it, but I think it was meant to be a meeting of the Nordic, or Aryan, nations."

"And Lucinda Robinson was there?"

"Yes. Speaking only German and treated as if she were another diplomat."

Mrs. Roosevelt, accompanied by Ed Kennelly and Dom Deconcini, entered the archives room a little after seven on Tuesday morning. The room was lighted only by morning sunlight shining on the windows, but that was more than light enough; the June sun had been up for hours and shone directly on the south windows. The room was in fact uncomfortably bright.

They had come to examine the room before the N.Y.A. archive workers would arrive for their day's work. The room was quiet. Papers lay in scattered heaps on all the desks, on shelves, and in cartons around the floor.

"I should think one of the closets a more likely place than any of the cabinets," said Mrs. Roosevelt.

"We examined the closets and the cabinets," said Deconcini. "A body that's dead of strangulation does not bleed, so there are no bloodstains."

"It's not bloodstains that I expect to find," said Mrs. Roosevelt.

She opened one of the closets and looked inside. It was filled with cartons of papers, stacked four deep. The second closet seemed to be used as a coat closet. It contained two umbrellas, a raincoat hanging from a bar, from which also hung a dozen wire hangers, and a hat on a shelf.

"All right," she said. "If poor Lucinda was placed in here— Do you see my point?"

"Excuse me," said Kennelly. He dropped to his hands and knees and peered hard at the wood floor of the closet. He shook his head. "I don't see any sign. Didn't expect to. But we can do the test. I brought what you asked for."

He reached for and opened a small case that he had carried from headquarters. It contained a pint bottle of distilled water and a roll of white blotting paper. When he unscrewed the cap, the bottle proved equipped with a shaker spout. He shook water onto the floor, spreading it over about half the area of the closet, in the center, not around the walls. He replaced the cap on the bottle and put it aside. Then he unrolled a length of the blotting paper and tore it into rough pieces, each about four inches square.

"Let it soak a bit," he said as he paused.

"That blotting paper has been treated with—?" Deconcini asked.

"I don't know," said Kennelly. "Something. The lab man said it was a reliable test."

He spread the blotting paper out on the floor. Two of the squares turned pink.

"There you have it," said Kennelly. "By golly, there's been urine on this floor. It's not necessarily hers, though. We have to remember that."

"But very likely hers," said Mrs. Roosevelt. "If her urinary tract relaxed in death and released enough urine to have stained her dress, it would be found on the floor where her body was left for at least thirty-six hours. Her clothes soaked up most of it, but some reached the floor and dried there."

"Even if the murderer tried to wipe it up," said Kennelly,

"he couldn't wipe up what soaked into the wood. But we have to face it. Somebody may have— Well, you know."

"Urinated in the closet," said the First Lady. "As long ago as the presidency of Andrew Jackson."

"Only since the wooden floor was last oiled, actually," said Kennelly.

He shook some more water on the floor, this time around the baseboard. The blotting paper used on that water came away showing no pink stain.

"I'm getting to be convinced," he said. "If someone had done it on the floor, it would have spread all over, that much of it. The test indicates urine on just a small area. I'm ready to say the body was here."

"All right," said Mrs. Roosevelt. "We know she was killed on Thursday, the morning when the King and Queen arrived. At that time, the young people of the N.Y.A. were not here. They were serving as maids and an usher. Wednesday afternoon, Thursday, and Friday. But Saturday morning they would be here again, and the body had to be moved."

"Why did it have to be moved?" asked Kennelly. "If it was going to be found Monday morning, anyway?"

"To be discovered," said Mrs. Roosevelt. "But I have began to entertain a pretty firm idea of who did it. And why."

Kennelly smiled at her. "And you won't tell us what you think, because you want us to figure it out for ourselves."

"I don't want you to accept my idea," she said. "I want to find evidence that brings you to the same conclusion."

Detective Sergeant Fred Mariott folded his newspaper and laid it aside on the marble bench where he had been sitting, on the banking floor of Farmers & Mechanics National Bank. He nodded to the bank guard, to whom he had earlier identified himself, and walked toward a man in a brown suit and brown hat who had just joined the line at one of the teller windows. The guard put his hand on his revolver and moved slowly closer to the man.

"You are David Lasky, I believe," said Mariott.

The man jerked his shoulders, and his jaw dropped. He watched fearfully as Mariott showed him a badge. Then he frowned and nodded.

"You are under arrest, sir," said Mariott, and he pulled a pair of handcuffs from his jacket pocket.

Mrs. Roosevelt was certain she was about to solve the mystery of the death of Lucinda Robinson, but she could not allow her eagerness to have the dismaying matter resolved to interfere with her duties as First Lady. At noon, when she would have liked to pursue a theory that had begun to dominate her mind, she was obliged to speak at a luncheon of the American Association of University Women.

Part of what she said was—

> Why must nations spend more and more and still more on weapons of war? We think we do it because we must, meaning because others are doing it. In truth, we must do it, even we the United States, lest we find ourselves a deficiently armed nation facing heavily armed aggressors. But proliferation of weapons has never prevented war, only encouraged it, as history shows, and I fear the danger of a new world war is very real and uncomfortably near.
>
> I have never been able to understand why the statesmen of the world cannot sit down around a conference table and resolve our chief differences. I suppose the reason why they can't is that the resolution of differences would require mutual concessions.
>
> For example, however much German and Italian misconduct may anger us, we must acknowledge that Germany and Italy were treated unfairly after the great war. The German people in particular were

shorn of their pride and left miserable. Difficult
though it may be for most of us to accept, I have to
wonder if reasonable concessions to the German nation before the advent of Herr Hitler, or maybe even
after, might have blunted the German drive for rear-
mament and territorial aggrandizement.

Ed Kennelly did not telephone the First Lady and report to
her the arrest of David Lasky. There would be time for that
after Kennelly interrogated him, and he had decided to have
the answers he wanted out of Lasky, by his own methods,
before Mrs. Roosevelt had a chance to plead for wishy-washy
questioning.

Lasky had been taken to the drunk tank immediately on
arriving at headquarters. The drunk tank was a simple cage
with a concrete floor and a drain in the center. The overnight
drunks had all been released by noon, and the cage had been
hosed down. Two officers stripped Lasky and sat him down
on a folding steel chair with his back to the bars of the cage.
They pulled his right arm out to the right and used a pair of
handcuffs to fasten it to a bar, then pulled his left arm to the
left and cuffed it to another bar. Naked and spread-eagled,
the terrified Lasky sat and waited.

Kennelly left him waiting for an hour before he came
down.

"Well, Lasky," he said. "Tried to absquatulate again, huh?
Only you had to have some dough. I figured you've have to
make a stop at the bank."

Lasky shook his head, as if acknowledging a mistake.

Kennelly stared contemptuously at the thin, oddly smooth,
hairless body of the young man. "Lessee. What made you decide to run again? I can guess, but why don't you tell me?"

Lasky shook his head. "There's nothing to tell. I decided I
was still a suspect and—"

"Won't do, Lasky," said Kennelly harshly. "And I don't

have much patience with you. Dammit, you tell me the straight story, and tell it now!"

"What else can I say?"

"Let's find out," said Kennelly.

He unrolled the canvas hose that was used to flush down the floor of the drunk tank. It was a fire hose with an adjustable nozzle that could shoot a spray or a stream. He turned the valve. Adjusting it halfway between stream and spray, he played the cold water on David Lasky.

Lasky shrieked and tried to tuck his chin under his right arm to protect his face. Kennelly turned the nozzle to shoot a stream, and shot an arm-thick blast of water against Lasky's belly, then into his crotch. Lasky struggled and knocked over his chair. He dropped to his knees on the floor. Kennelly turned off the water.

Lasky shivered and groaned. Kennelly hung up the hose and leaned against the wall while he lit a cigarette.

Lasky began to sob, and he mumbled, "I don't have anything to do with it. I was played for a sucker."

"About what?" asked Kennelly mock casually.

"About the key."

"What I figured. Why the hell didn't you just say so and save yourself a lot of grief?"

David Lasky wept. "What's this going to cost me?" he asked. "Jail and disbarment and—"

"Maybe not, if you quit lying. You can buy yourself some sympathy and maybe some help, if you tell the whole story."

Lasky hung his head and nodded.

Kennelly stepped into the hall outside and said, "Madge . . ." Then he set up the folding chair again and helped Lasky to get up and sit on it.

Madge was the police stenographer, a woman with the face of a boxer and a body to match, carrying a fistful of yellow pencils and a steno pad. "F' Chrissake, Kennelly! Cover him up!"

"I've got nothin' to cover him with. You're a grown-up girl. You want to tell me that son of yours isn't like him?"

"Not quite," said Madge. She sat down at a small square wooden table and laid out her steno pad. "Shoot."

Kennelly began by asking Lasky his name, age, occupation, place of employment, and place of residence. Then he said, "Do you make this statement of your own free will, free of any compulsion?"

Lasky nodded.

"Out loud, son," said Madge.

"Yes."

"Tell us about the key," said Kennelly.

"The key to the tunnel? Mr. Hopkins had a key. One morning there were some pickets across the street from the White House, and Mr. Hopkins said to me, 'Come on, and I'll show you how to get out of here in private.' And he took me through the Treasury tunnel. After that, I asked him once if I could use the key. He said sure. So I used it to impress Lucinda. I wanted her to think I was a big, important guy in the White House. Then one day she asked me if she could use the key. I told her she couldn't, that I didn't dare let anyone else use it. But . . . Well, by then I was in love with her. I mean, I thought I couldn't live without her. The old story, huh?"

"Let's put some times on this," said Kennelly. "When did you first date Lucinda Robinson?"

"In December."

"Didn't you know she was seeing other men?"

Lasky nodded, but seeing Madge glare he spoke. "Yes. But I thought she quit seeing other men. I thought I was the only man she was seeing for a while."

"When was that?"

"From, say, February until maybe early in May."

"We talked about Charles Pitt. She was seeing him, too,

during that time. Also a man named Martin Willoughby. You didn't know? Really?"

Lasky hung his head. "No," he whispered. "I thought she was just seeing me, until the Kraut came along."

"Get back to the key," said Kennelly.

"She kept asking for the key. Uh . . . you can't imagine how persuasive she could be. The girl was . . . I don't know what to call her."

"So you gave her the key."

"Yes, and then she didn't bring it back. She'd promised she would—"

"She tried to have it copied," said Kennelly. "And couldn't."

"She didn't tell me that. I was in a panic. Mr. Hopkins's key was gone, and God only knew what she wanted with it!"

"We know now."

"Yes, but that's all I had to do with it! I swear! I was fool enough to give her the key."

"And fool enough to write letters threatening to kill her."

"That too," Lasky admitted weakly.

Kennelly stared at him for a moment, then said, "All right. You're going in the lockup. You're afraid of that, so we'll put you in an individual cell. Jeez, you could have saved yourself a lot of trouble if you'd come square with me from the beginning."

Mrs. Roosevelt sighed. "Thank you, Ed. I had guessed it, as you had. I feel terribly sorry for the young man. You say you've put him in a separate cell, so that others will not be able to hurt him?"

They were alone in her office. Baines and Deconcini were on their way up but had not arrived.

"Lasky had a shower," said Kennelly. "He got into a nice clean pair of coveralls. And now he's comfortably locked up in his own private cell."

"The crime of taking that key . . . That's not so terrible, is it?"

Kennelly shrugged. "Petty larceny."

"We may have to keep the fact from Mr. Hoover," she said with a sly smile.

"No problem."

"I have an idea," she said. "I think we should look into the digs of Mr. Christian Cassell."

"Happy to," said Kennelly. "Wanta say why?"

"He has aroused a suspicion," she said. "He told us he had never been anywhere but the ground floor of the White House—and that almost exclusively in the east end of it—during all the time he has worked here, except for the time when he served as a temporary usher for the royal visit. But Missy LeHand tells me she has seen him in the West Wing. He lied about that."

"What'll we find in his digs?" asked Kennelly. "If he's what you think he might be, a German spy, you can be sure he doesn't keep any evidence of it in his rooms."

"What I would like to know," said Mrs. Roosevelt, "is whether or not the photographs taken with the Minox camera, showing a room where someone was apparently experimenting with the camera, are photographs of Mr. Cassell's room."

Kennelly chuckled. "My very dear lady," he said, "you would have made a fine detective."

Half an hour later Mrs. Roosevelt led Greta Bergstrom, wife of the Swedish ambassador, on a brief tour of the White House. It was not a social or diplomatic tour. It was purposeful.

They paused at the door of the room where the N.Y.A. group was still working on the Wilson archives.

"These young people are working in the White House under the auspices of the National Youth Administration,"

Mrs. Roosevelt explained to Mrs. Bergstrom. "They are sorting and indexing some of the wartime papers of President Wilson."

As they walked back along the hall, toward the elevator that would take them upstairs for tea, Mrs. Bergstrom said, "He is the man. I have no doubt of it at all. That young man, working there in the archives room, was the young man I saw escorting Lucinda Robinson at the German Embassy."

At four o'clock a small group met in the Monroe Room on the second floor. Present were: the First Lady, Director Hoover, Agent Willoughby, Captain Kennelly, Senior Agent Baines, and Agent Deconcini.

"The identification by Mrs. Bergstrom is most suggestive," said Mrs. Roosevelt. "But I believe the fact that the photographs on the first part of the Minox film are pictures of Mr. Cassell's room is really conclusive. Either Mary Logan or Lucinda Robinson took those photographs. I am more inclined to believe it was Lucinda than Mary. The fingerprints on the film cartridge are Lucinda's."

Hoover scratched his ear. "The time has come to arrest Cassell," he said.

Mrs. Roosevelt nodded. "What precaution can you take to be sure he does not kill himself with poison, the way Mary Logan did?"

"We can handle that," said Kennelly grimly. "I suggest you don't come with us and watch us take him. It's going to be a little rough."

"Bring him to this room," said the First Lady. "I'll ask Miss Thompson to take shorthand notes of his interrogation."

They did not take Cassell in the archives room. They waited until he came out.

Deconcini and Willoughby stepped quickly behind him

and grabbed his arms. Kennelly rushed in front and smashed a fist into Cassell's mouth, and Baines instantly jammed a wooden toilet-paper roller between his teeth.

Cassell could not bite down, and Kennelly searched inside his mouth with a finger. He found no capsule.

They took him to the physician's office and stripped him. They found no poison. They let him dress again, cuffed his hands behind his back, and took him upstairs to confront the First Lady.

Kennelly's punch had bloodied Cassell's mouth, and since his hands were cuffed behind his back, he could not wipe away the tiny trickle of it that issued from his split lower lip. The blood was drying on his chin. His pale blue eyes glittered. He sat stiffly upright, furious and defiant.

Extra chairs had been carried into the Monroe Room, and Tommy Thompson sat at a little table with a supply of pencils and shorthand pads.

"Are you ready to tell the truth?" asked J. Edgar Hoover.

"About what?" asked Cassell. "With what heinous offense do you charge me?"

"Espionage," said Hoover dramatically.

"Actually," said Mrs. Roosevelt, "I believe the more serious charge will be the murder of Miss Lucinda Robinson. You will be hanged for that, Mr. Cassell."

Cassell's jaw trembled. His eyes widened. He shook his head. "No . . ." he muttered.

Mrs. Roosevelt raised her hand to cut short a question by Hoover. In truth, they had no real evidence that Cassell had committed the murder, only evidence that he was a German spy. What they needed was a confession. Cassell appeared to be afraid. Maybe she could take advantage of that and get the confession.

"Your only chance of escaping the noose, Mr. Cassell, is

cooperation. Even that may not save you, but it is your only chance. Hanging is an ugly way to die."

Kennelly's lips parted. He frowned. He had not imagined that Mrs. Roosevelt, usually so ready to extend sympathy, so unwilling to wound, had the steely resolution to pounce on this man's fear and confusion and reinforce them by reminding him that hanging is a painful way to die.

Cassell frowned and nodded rhythmically for a full minute, where everyone stared at him in accusing silence. Then he said, "All right. I did kill her." His chin shot up, and his eyes hardened. "I had to do it! It was my duty!"

"What is your name?" asked Mrs. Roosevelt. "And where are you from?"

"My name is Kurt von Keyserling, *Hauptsturmführer SS*. I am from Berlin."

"And Ana Becker, known in America as Mary Logan, worked for you?"

"Yes."

"When she was caught, she killed herself," said Kennelly. "We thought you'd try the same thing. That's why you got the shot on the mouth."

"I understood," said von Keyserling. *"Fraulein* Becker was a complete fanatic. I am of a more practical turn of mind."

"Tell us about Lucinda," said Mrs. Roosevelt.

"She was . . . an immoral woman," said von Keyserling. "I did not have to seduce her. She— Well, we need not discuss the details. I had a job in the White House, as did Ana, but—"

"Who in the N.Y.A. arranged that for you?" Hoover asked.

"Nobody," said von Keyserling. "Ana applied for her job and got it. Then I applied, and it was quite easy to get the job, since I could read German and some of the documents were in German. We were able to convince the screening officers at the N.Y.A. that we were would-be university students looking for jobs that would enable us to continue our education."

"There is no German agent in the N.Y.A.?" Hoover asked.

Von Keyserling smiled sarcastically. "No. You won't find us everywhere. I had hoped that having jobs in the White House would make it possible for Ana and me to move about the premises and observe things. But we were instructed to remain in the east end of the ground floor. I broke that rule, but I could not do it often. I needed another agent, someone who could go anywhere in the White House. Lucinda could do that. So I sought her company and won her affection—a task that was easy."

"She wrote her parents that she might soon be marrying a man with a title of nobility," said Mrs. Roosevelt.

"Yes. I am *von* Keyserling. Though titles mean little today, I am Baron von Keyserling. Lucy was fascinated with the idea that she might become a baroness. Also, she wanted to enter the diplomatic service. I indicated to her that I could probably arrange that for her—though it might be the *German* diplomatic service. I suggested to her that she and I might be appointed to represent the Third Reich in some country or other, perhaps in Asia, perhaps in South America."

"Did you promise to marry her?"

"She assumed it. I did not discourage her."

"You took her to a reception at the German Embassy."

"I shouldn't have, but it was necessary. I needed to dazzle her. I called at the embassy, identified myself, and arranged for Lucy and me to be received as honored guests. The embassy cooperated."

"You needed to dazzle her," Mrs. Roosevelt repeated thoughtfully. "To recruit her into your service."

"Yes."

"How did you get the key to the Treasury tunnel?"

"Lucy got it for me."

"How? From whom?" asked Mrs. Roosevelt.

"I don't know how. At that time she was still playing a game. She was . . . like a child. To get the key was to her just some fun. She actually allowed that fool Schoenberg to escort her to meetings of the German-American Bund. When I learned that, I forbade her to go to any more such meetings, to avoid the identification."

"You taught her to use the Minox camera."

"Yes."

"You made a fatal error there, Herr von Keyserling. The pictures she took while learning remained on the film that was in the camera when Ana used it to photograph maps and documents in the situation room."

Von Keyserling frowned hard. "So—" he said curtly.

"You say you had to kill her. Why?"

He sighed loudly. "The game began to frighten her. When she understood I had taught her to use the camera, also to pick locks, so we could enter the situation room and photograph the maps, she became panicky. For days she would not talk to me. Then she demanded I return the key. And finally . . ." He sighed again. "Finally she began to talk about returning the key and confessing why she had taken it." He shook his head. "I couldn't allow her to do that."

"You killed her on Thursday morning, the day the King and Queen arrived," said Mrs. Roosevelt.

"I telephoned her and told her to come into the archives room and I would give her the key. Everyone was gone from there. They had all gone upstairs. She came in. I asked her for a kiss. She said I must give her the key first. I did, and while she was staring at it to be sure it was the right one, I stepped behind her and strangled her—as I had intended to do."

"You hid her body in the coat closet," said Mrs. Roosevelt. "Why did you later have to move it?"

"Coat closet? What makes you think . . . ?" He shrugged. "I guess you know all. What difference does it make?"

"Why did you have to move it?" Mrs. Roosevelt persisted.

"It would have been found on Saturday morning, when we returned to our regular work on the Wilson papers. I reported to my superiors that—"

"How do you report to your superiors?" Hoover demanded.

"By radio. I transmit at regular intervals. In fact, I was supposed to transmit at six o'clock, which obviously I have not done. This means that my code is no longer valid."

"Where do you transmit your messages to?" Hoover asked.

"You may find this hard to believe, Mr. Director Hoover," said von Keyserling, "but I don't know where the transmissions are received. Maybe in Canada or Mexico, or maybe on a ship at sea. Maybe in West Virginia. I don't know. My messages are received somewhere and relayed to Berlin by a more powerful transmitter, probably in a different code."

"Where is this transmitter?"

"In a room I rent in a house on Florida Avenue. One of the keys you took from me is the key to that room."

"I am still mystified as to why you had to move the body," said Mrs. Roosevelt.

"I sent my report that Thursday evening. Very quickly I got a reply, asking where I had hidden the body and when it would be found. I was instructed to reply and wait for further instructions. I waited for an hour, almost, and then an angry message came through. My superiors were angry at me for murdering Lucy when the King and Queen of England were in Washington. They ordered me to move the body to where it could not be found until the King and Queen were away from Washington, or better after they had left the United States."

"Why?" asked Hoover. "What difference did it make when the body was found?"

"They said the discovery that a murder had been committed in the White House when the King and Queen were there—though actually they had not arrived at the hour when I did it—would be an immense embarrassment to President Roosevelt, who would be driven to do something 'compensatory.' That is the word they used: 'compensatory.' I suppose they meant the President would be driven to make some sort of gesture, likely in the form of promising closer cooperation between the United States and the British warmongers."

"So you moved her, on Friday night," said Mrs. Roosevelt.

"Yes. I knew the White House schedule—partly because Lucy had given me much information about it when she still thought she was playing a game. I knew I could hide the body in a linen closet, because the dirty linen would not be removed from there before Monday morning."

"Couldn't you have carried the body somewhere not so far away, not so difficult?" Baines asked.

"This was the easiest place. I thought about it a long time and decided how to move her."

"You'd never been on the third floor, I assume," said Mrs. Roosevelt. "Even if you knew the linen would not be taken down to the laundry before Monday morning, how did you know where the linen closet was?"

Von Keyserling smiled again, a bitter little smile. "My very good Lucy had provided me with floor plans of every floor in the White House and its adjacent wings. I had memorized those plans carefully and thoroughly. I know for example which third-floor rooms belong to Miss LeHand. I know which ones used to belong to Mr. Howe. I can find my way around the White House. If you elect to go to war against my country, Mrs. President Roosevelt, you will find that we Germans are formidable for our ability to do our work skillfully."

"How did you move the body?" Hoover asked.

Von Keyserling glanced at Mrs. Roosevelt. "I imagine the lady knows," he said. "I returned to the White House through

the tunnel—having picked a simple lock on a door of the
Treasury Building. I pushed her out the window of the archives room, after midnight. Then I went to the third floor
and out on the promenade, from where I lowered a rope. I
looped that rope around her and returned to the promenade.
I raised her to the roof, carried her inside, and left her in the
linen closet. I could have left her out on the grounds, of
course, but it seemed to me the message to the White House
would be more emphatic if I left her on the third floor."

"Message?"

"That you can't hide from us. That we are everywhere.
That even if you hang me, my comrades will destroy you. For
we are the men of a superior race! A superior nation! We cannot lose! *Heil Hitler!*"

EPILOGUE

Kurt von Keyserling, *Hauptsturmführer SS*, entered a plea of guilty to premeditated murder. Because he had confessed and because he cooperated fully in keeping the whole matter a secret, he was spared hanging and was sentenced to life imprisonment. He was imprisoned at Alcatraz from 1939 to 1948, when he was transferred to Leavenworth. In 1964, having served twenty-five years, he was released. He did not return to Germany but lived in Cleveland, Ohio, where he found work as a locksmith. He died in 1989 at the age of 75.

Director J. Edgar Hoover prepared a self-congratulatory press release, telling how he had uncovered a German spy ring inside the White House, and was deeply disappointed when the President issued to him a direct order not to release it and instead to keep the entire matter confidential.

David Lasky was released from jail the day after von Keyserling confessed. He resigned his job at the White House but was not charged with any crime or disbarred as he had feared. He went to Florida and lived there with his father for a time. Late in 1940, he was drafted into the United States Army. In spite of his fragile physique, he was trained to be a combat infantryman. He served with distinction in North Africa and Sicily, was wounded, and was transferred to the Judge Advocate General Corps in early 1944, with the rank of captain. After the war he joined a law firm in Philadelphia, where he became a senior partner, then managing partner. He never married but kept a mistress, to whom he left his entire estate when he died in 1979.

Of Lucinda Robinson's other lovers, only Charles Pitt left any history. Too old to be drafted, he used his father's political influence to obtain for himself a naval commission in 1942. Commander Pitt was aboard the cruiser *Indianapolis* when it delivered the atomic bomb to Tinian—and was one of very few men on board who knew what it was. A few days later he was killed when the *Indianapolis* was sunk by a Japanese submarine.

On August 24, a few days more than two months after Mrs. Roosevelt extracted the confession from Kurt von Keyserling, Nazi Germany and Soviet Russia signed a non-aggression pact, including secret clauses that divided Poland between them.

On September 1, 1939, Germany invaded Poland.